THE

LEVER DU CINÉ COLLECTION :

RENAISSANCE

LEVER DU CINÉ

Copyright © 2024 Lever du Ciné

All rights reserved. No part of this publication may be reproduced, distributed, or transmitted in any form or by any means, including photocopying, recording, filming, or other electronic or mechanical methods, without the prior written permission of the author, except as permitted by U.S. copyright law.

For permission requests, please contact leverducine@gmail.com.

Paperback ISBN: 979-8-871-46972-9

Hardcover ISBN: 979-8-871-46992-7

Cover art: *The Valley of the Dee, with Chester in the Distance (1761)* by Richard Wilson (1714-1782)

To my loving and supportive parents and siblings

To my closest friends

To Alessia

And to those who have supported me on my journey
leading to this recorded point in human history

I love you

CONTENTS

Royal Posture	1
Enantiodromia	11
There Was a Knock at the Door 1 2 3	41
The Bunker	71

Cullen Castle, Banffshire (between 1770-1780) by Robert Adam (1728-1792)

Royal Posture

Written by

Lever du Ciné

SUPERIMPOSE: "There was an acquired taste in the air..."

FADE IN ON...

EXT. TOLLYMORE FOREST – FOGGY DAWN

A quiet green forest sits within a mist.

MUSIC CUE: ["SYMPHONY NO. 6 IN B MINOR, OP. 74 'PATHETIQUE' ADAGIO LAMENTOSO" BY PYTOR TCHAIKOVSKY]

INT. MODERN ROOM – DAY

Georgian decor fills a large modern room.

SLOW DOLLY IN: on the center of the room, where a man (30s, English, in an apparent state of decay) lies on a white couch, dressed in Georgian fashion. This is FARROW. He methodically stirs a negroni cocktail as he stares lost into the distance.

A middle-aged maid dressed in modern business attire enters the room. She stands over him as he continues to zone out.

> THE MAID
> Farrow. Supper is ready. The family has requested you come eat with them in the dinning quarters.

No reply.

> THE MAID
> Would you like to take it in here or in the quarters?

No reply again.

Farrow melancholically looks at a painting hanging on a wall across the room: a sad young man sits on a bench in a park feeding birds.

> THE MAID
> Farrow, should I have the dinning quarters prepared for you or –

Farrow wildly tosses the drink into the air.

                            FARROW
                      (shouting hysterically)
              Dammit! You fool! Prepare the bloody table!
           Am I paying you to repeatedly ask these questions woman?
              How can I willingly live on knowing you are bloody here,
               with the sole existence to waste every waking second of –

INT. CASTLE HALLWAY – DAY

A long castle hallway sits pristine, and empty.

INT. MODERN DINING HALL – DAY

In a massive dining room, a dozen people (dressed in modern clothing) sit at a long table eating. Farrow is seated at the head of the table. He stirs a drink as the people around him laugh and eat like animals.

A manservant approaches Farrow with a platter, resting it on the table. He lifts the lid - a HUMAN HEART sits on the tray, hot and steamy. Next to it is a note: **The Maid**.

Farrow picks at the heart, taking nibbles.

                         TENSINGTON *(O.S.)*
                        (faintly, getting louder)
                    Farrow… Farrow… Farrow… Farrow!

                            FARROW
                          (irritated)
                             What!

An older woman sits a few seats away. This is TENSINGTON.

                          TENSINGTON
                 Farrow, that's your third one this month.

Another middle-aged woman (black hair) across the table stops her conversation and turns to them. This is LYDIA.

                            LYDIA
                  Third one? Farrow is that your third one?

ROYAL POSTURE

> TENSINGTON
> Farrow that can't be good for your iron levels. Farrow.

A shaking, confused elderly lady drops her spoon.

> GRANDMA JULIE
> When is Farrow arriving for supper?

> TENSINGTON
> He's here now mother.

> WESTERHOFF
> Grand ma ma, he's at the end of the table! Look across.

> GRANDMA JULIE
> Oh, oh…

Farrow covers his head in frustration.

> FARROW
> Can you please just let me eat my supper in peace. Please.

A middle-aged man looks across.

> HENRY
> *(sardonically)*
> If he stays in this bitter mood we are going to run out of help to hire.

The table bursts into laughter and chatter. Farrow closes his eyes, zoning out as he eats the heart. His name is mentioned repeatedly. Within the haze…

> LITTLE JOHNNY BOY *(O.S.)*
> *(whisper)*
> Today we are going to kill you.

Beat. Farrow opens his eyes and looks around the table.

> FARROW
> *(screaming)*
> Quiet!

The table falls silent. Farrow finds the boy on the other end.

                    FARROW
        My dear boy, what did you just say?

The little boy stares at him with such innocence.

                LITTLE JOHNNY BOY
        I said, '*today we are going to kill you.*'

IMMEDIATELY – everyone draws a knife, pointing at him.

Farrow sits, motionless.

                    WESTERHOFF
        Farrow, we are here today to issue
        your removal from this Monarchy.

Farrow looks around at all the faces at the table, before taking a bite of the heart.

                    FARROW
              On what charge?

                    LYDIA
            Call it: vain negligence.

                    FARROW
        And do you all feel this way about my tenancy's demise?

They stare silently. Farrow placatingly nods, cleaning his mess.

                    FARROW
            So… It is treason then.

No answer. Farrow slams his hand on the table standing up.

                    FARROW
                  (screaming)
    Treason?! After all I've done for this empire? After what you…
                (overcome with emotion)
        After what you did to my wife in order to
        remove her, you have the audacity to –

WESTERHOFF
Do not forget Farrow, that you were
just as involved in that as we were.

Disgusted, Farrow turns to Grandma Julie.

FARROW
Even you grand ma ma? You'd do this to your beloved
sweet bonbon boy? Do you forget all those moments
I would sit by your bed as a mere child and you would tell
me stories of the olden days, and when we would bake
sweet cakes together for the other children of the manor?
Or when you would bathe me inside the florescent –

GRANDMA JULIE
(confused)
When is Farrow getting here?

Everyone turns to her.

FAMILY ENSEMBLE	**FARROW**
He's right here Grandmother.	I'm right bloody here ma ma!

GRANDMA JULIE
Oh, oh… right…

Grandma Julie re-points her knife at him with a serious demeanor.

FARROW
You know what you little twits, I shall not stand for this!
For the last four years I provided you with everything
you could have ever wanted! More than Sarah ever did.

LYDIA
Your claim to the throne is illegitimate. You gained through
marriage. We all know I was supposed to be the next in line.

FARROW
Oh shut it Lydia, your tits are illegitimate.
Let me know when you're going to give round
three of Botox a go. I'll make sure to chip in.

DING DONG! The tension in the room is sliced by the elaborate doorbell.

A manservant enters.

                    THE MANSERVANT
                There is a parcel for you, Sir.

Farrow nervously watches the faces around the table – knives still pointed towards him. He re-sits.

                          FARROW
                        Send them in.

The Manservant exits, and a Deliveryman enters. He approaches Farrow with a large square package.

                   THE DELIVERYMAN
           I've got a package for the Dinkley Estate…?

Without looking away from the table, Farrow signs for it. The Deliveryman looks around at the obscure scene.

                   THE DELIVERYMAN
             Cheers mate, have a nice day.

He exits. Farrow timidly eyes the package.

                          FARROW
                       (nervously)
                Is this what I think it is?

                          HENRY
                     It 'tis indeed.

Little Johnny Boy gets up and approaches the box. He methodically cuts it open and pulls out its content: a CROWN – fit just for him.

                      TENSINGTON
                    (mesmerized)
                    It's wonderful.

Everyone watches Little Johnny Boy carefully place the crown on his head. Farrow looks on with an almost reminiscing disgust.

ROYAL POSTURE

                    WESTERHOFF
                A handsome young King.

Farrow jumps up and sprints down the long room towards the exit. Everyone at the table sits and watches.

INT. CASTLE – CONTINUOUS

SERIES OF WIDE SHOTS: as Farrow sprints alone through various Georgian styled rooms in the castle, panting wildly.

He passes through a HIGH TECH SERVER ROOM.

INT. MODERN ROOM – CONTINUOUS

Farrow enters into his quarters. He leans over his sofa trying to catch his breath.

SHING! Blood splatters over the white couch. Farrow looks down at his stomach and sees a blade sticking through him. He turns - Little Johnny Boy stands behind him.

                     FARROW
            Why… why have you done this to me my son?

                LITTLE JOHNNY BOY
              Father, it's just how it has to be.

The rest of the large family circle around him. Little Johnny Boy goes to plow in his knife again, however, something catches Farrow's eye.

                     FARROW
                      Wait!

They halt. Farrow looks past the boy towards the painting on the wall: the young man on the bench is now elderly. He smiles and holds a bird in his hands, with tears in his eyes.

Farrow, likewise, is now in tears.

                    FARROW
                    (smiling)
                  I see you now.

Little Johnny Boy and the family move in and begin to stab him over, and over, and over again...

INT. MODERN DINING HALL – CONTINUOUS

The unfinished human heart sits on the dining table. Faint sounds of the continued stabbings are heard far off.

                                        FADE TO BLACK

SUPERIMPOSE TEXT: **"Alas, the end of a monarchy... and the disposition of vanity."**

                                        ROLL CREDITS

                                            THE END

The Great Fire of London in 1666 (between 1666-1686) by Lieve Verschuier (1627-1686)

Enantiodromia

Written by

Lever du Ciné

ENANTIODROMIA

MUSIC CUE: ["PIANO CONCERTO NO.2 IN C MINOR, OP.18: II. ADAGIO SOSTENUTO" BY SERGEI RACHMANINOFF]

FADE IN ON...

INT. WAREHOUSE OFFICE – DAY

CLOSE UP: of an old TV. The screen statics as a news intro appears. An anchor sits at a desk.

> NEWS ANCHOR JANET
> Good afternoon Los Angeles this is Janet from Channel 24 WLT News, with your afternoon broadcast. Tensions are rising in downtown as today's Fascist rally was rather violently interrupted by Antifa protesters; who threw balloons filled with nair and horse urine on the ralliers as they repeatedly chanted "Mickey must die".

Footage appears of an older white man in a suit being escorted away from the chaos by security guards.

> NEWS ANCHOR JANET *(cont'd)*
> This in clear reference to Mickey Dowinger who is currently running for presidency in the increasingly popular Fascist party. Matters only further escalated when a different protest group – now identified as the Anti-Anti-Fascists – came onto the scene and began inciting hostilities towards the Antifa rioters. A reminder for new viewers just now tuning in to the situation, The Anti-Anti-Fascists do not consider themselves Pro Fascist, but simply Anti, Anti-Fascists.

INT. HALLWAYS, WAREHOUSE – CONTINUOUS

TRACKING: through the winding corridors of the warehouse...

> NEWS ANCHOR JANET *(V.O.)*
> LAPD arrived to the scene promptly in attempt to control the three way conflict... however this seemed to only further escalate the chaos, to the point where Los Angeles Police Commissioner Sterling has deemed the situation a 'city wide emergency'.

THE LEVER DU CINÉ COLLECTION : RENAISSANCE

… Past a break room with a TV. On it, an image appears next to Janet – of JOHN WITHERSPOON (black, 30s, calm demeanor).

>   NEWS ANCHOR JANET
> We've received reports that the head of the A.A.F. movement –
> John Witherspoon, seen here – has disappeared during the
> chaos, with police believing Antifa to be responsible.

Down a hall towards an open double set of doors…

>   NEWS ANCHOR JANET *(V.O.)*
> We are being told by police that there are a couple of
> suspects in question but no leads as of yet. When any
> new information is presented we'll make sure you,
> our viewers, are first to know…

INT. WAREHOUSE – CONTINUOUS

The music echoes inside a large empty warehouse.

In the middle of the room is a body tied to a chair (facing profile) with a bag over their head and a noose around their neck, connected to the high ceiling.

>   BAGGED FIGURE
>   *(voice choked and unrecognizable)*
>   Enantiodromia… Enantiodromia…
>   Enantiodromia… Enantiodromia…

A squeaky door opens far off. The bagged figure TURNS TO CAMERA.

>   BAGGED FIGURE *(cont'd)*
>   Dammit.

Two men in ski masks rapidly approach the victim.

A Japanese man (40s, with bifocals, a bit bigger in frame) slams the chair back as a younger man (white, 20s) begins to slowly pour water on the victim's face with a hose. These are SHIGOTO and JIM THE ENTERTAINER respectively.

The bagged figure shakes violently as they gasp for breath.

ENANTIODROMIA

JIM THE ENTERTAINER
You hearing this? The opening is the best part man.
It's like… it's what they call subtle.

He closes his eyes and hums to the rhythm.

SHIGOTO
(spoken in Japanese)
You know nothing about the art of classical progression –

JIM THE ENTERTAINER
English please.

SHIGOTO
You so wrong. The ending issa best part. The emotion composed into final portion is truly something special.

JIM THE ENTERTAINER
Agree to disagree.

SHIGOTO
You know, Rachmaninov compose this during hypnotherapy.

JIM THE ENTERTAINER
What? No way.

SHIGOTO
Yes, it is true. He was got very bad depression, and during hypnosis he wrote this. More amazing, no?

JIM THE ENTERTAINER
Nah that's crazy…

The bagged figure slowly stops moving as Shigoto and Jim the Entertainer lose themselves to the music.

SHIGOTO
It's almost like a cry of heart, beckoning for an answer amongst the chaos. Beckoning for a pause in the great, big bowel of –

JIM THE ENTERTAINER
Wait… How long were we supposed to run this again?

He cuts the water flow. The body is motionless. Jim the Entertainer and Shigoto exchange a look.

> JIM THE ENTERTAINER
> *(awkwardly joking)*
> Looks like you're not gonna get to the
> finale this time Shigoto. Music off.

The classical music cuts. Jim the Entertainer leans in close and puts his ear to the body's face. A beat.

The body JOLTS to life, coughing profusely. Relief falls on eyes of the men.

> JIM THE ENTERTAINER
> Mi amiga, are you ready to speak?

The choked person nods rapidly. Shigoto removes the bag – a Hispanic woman (30s) is revealed, her face without makeup, soaked, and red. This is KATE.

He removes the noose as she is finally given freedom to breathe.`

> KATE
> *(choked)*
> Listen… Listen I don't know what you want
> from me. I was just at the protest. I was just –

SHIGOTO	JIM THE ENTERTAINER
He no want to hear that…	*(quickly after)*
	I don't want to hear that
	again Kate.

> JIM THE ENTERTAINER *(cont'd)*
> Kate. We saw you with John at the rally. We know you're his accomplice.

SHIGOTO	JIM THE ENTERTAINER
You his right hand man…	*(quickly after)*
	You're his goddamn right hand
	woman Kate.

> JIM THE ENTERTAINER *(cont'd)*
> Come on, let's cut all the nonsense.

KATE
Please… Please I don't know what you're talking about just let me go. Just let me go! I'll do anything, I won't talk, I'll pay you whatever you want please!

Jim shakes his head in frustration.

JIM THE ENTERTAINER
Bag. Noose.

KATE
(welling up)
No… No please…

Shigoto picks up the bag and grabs the noose.

SHIGOTO
Bag. Noose.

KATE
No please, listen to me! Listen to me! No, no…

Shigoto goes to place the noose around her neck. Kate moves her head around trying to resist.

JIM THE ENTERTAINER
There's an easier way for us to go about all this,
but if you're not willing to play by our –

KATE
Alright!

The men freeze. Kate looks to them... and grins.

KATE
Alright. No fooling you. I really have to hand it to you Anti-Fascists, you all may be ignorant as hell but I mean wow, you're equally as stubborn.

JIM THE ENTERTAINER
Kate, Kate, Kate. Welcome. You see how easy this will be for the three of us now that we're all on the same page? Shigoto, tell her how easy.

SHIGOTO
(implicitly)
Very easy.

JIM THE ENTERTAINER
See that? *Very easy.* All it takes is a little cooperation. Some team play.

KATE
(harshly)
Screw you.

JIM THE ENTERTAINER
Whoa don't get all nasty now. There's still a chance for us to be good friends, okay? Now let's try this a little differently, shall we? My Antifa partner here goes by Shigoto. I am your host, Jim the Entertainer. And with your help, we're prepared to put on a fine show. Give us exactly what we ask for and I assure you you'll be free to walk out those doors and on your way. How's that sound?

KATE
Come on boys…

Her friendly demeanor slowly fades. She lunges towards them.

KATE
(ferociously)
Boys!

Both men flinch in a slight moment of fear.

KATE
You aren't cut for this line of work. This is a federal Offense you have on your hands here, you know that?
(to Jim the Entertainer)
You're some college punk that's way in over his head right now – I can see the USC initials on that hoodie you clearly just turned inside out by the way…
(to Shigoto)
…and judging by your – and no disrespect – *abysmal English*, I don't think trouble with the law is something you really need on your plate either.

ENANTIODROMIA

JIM THE ENTERTAINER
You have a lot of confidence for someone that's tied to a chair.

KATE
Yeah that's because I know something you don't. *Jim.*

JIM THE ENTERTAINER
Oh yeah? And that is?

KATE
(demeaningly)
Mr. Entertainer Boy, a secret has no worth if it's spoken.

JIM THE ENTERTAINER
Oh! That is precisely what we're here for though, isn't it? You know things that we don't. Well, it would be fair to say that we have a little secret of our own, don't we Shigoto?

SHIGOTO
We do, Jim.

JIM THE ENTERTAINER
Would you happened to know what our little secret is?

KATE
(sarcastically)
Don't believe I caught it with all that
water being poured down my throat.

Shigoto furiously slams her chair to the floor. Jim the Entertainer forces a REVOLVER to her skull.

JIM THE ENTERTAINER
You are disposable to us!

He cocks the gun. Kate closes her eyes in a quick cold fear. The trigger clicks and then -- **BLANK** No bullet.

JIM THE ENTERTAINER
And you hold no cards! In case you want to live to see another beach-side sunset I advise you to tell us what we want, when we want it. Got that?

As she opens her eyes, she spots a NAIL sticking up from the ground directly in front of her.

                JIM THE ENTERTAINER
                   Shigoto. Please.

Shigoto pulls Kate back up. She glances down at the nail.

                JIM THE ENTERTAINER
           Don't worry lil birdie, you won't get
            one of these as long as you chirp.

Jim fills the revolver with six bullets, then cocks the gun.

                JIM THE ENTERTAINER
       So. I shall ask you now: where can we find your
      good ole pal John Witherspoon, huh? He disappeared
      earlier today and we sure as hell know Antifa didn't
      nab him, because then we wouldn't be here, would we?

                      KATE
                  (exhaustedly)
              I honestly don't know.

                JIM THE ENTERTAINER
              Kate I swear to –

                      KATE
     You ever think there might be a slim possibility that
    he – oh I don't know – went home early from the riots?
Maybe stopped for a cup of Joe after a good ole Anti-Anti protest?

                JIM THE ENTERTAINER
       A good ole... Sorry, have you seen what's
      been happening out there or is it just me?
      Shigoto please tell me it's not just me man.

                    SHIGOTO
             Issa not just you.

ENANTIODROMIA

JIM THE ENTERTAINER
(exasperatedly)
The Anti-Fascists were the ones having a nice time protesting the scum Fascist rally, when you Anti-Anti-Fascists came in with your riots and all your Anti-Anti –

KATE
Okay please, enough of hearing you speak.
(to Shigoto)
Hi, shigoto, right?

Shigoto quickly and politely bows.

KATE
I know why this idiot is here, but you don't strike me as someone with his level of American ignorance.

SHIGOTO
No ma'am I am not ignorant, like American, I am from Japan.

KATE
Japan? Really?

Jim watches the two in disbelief of such casual conversation.

SHIGOTO
Yes, really. Japan is beautiful country, but one under terrible fascist rule. I fled with my wife and children here; for I can give them better life.

KATE
(sincerely)
Good for you Shigoto.

SHIGOTO
Yes yes, thank you. It was very big decision for my family. But now, fascist politician Mickey Dowinger is running to lead America. I did not take my family away from fascist country, to go to other fascist country. Would be crazy, no?

KATE
Believe me, I may be opposed to your methods, but I'm on your side there. You do the best for your family, I can see that.

Shigoto is strangely touched by this.

> SHIGOTO
> Thank you Kate...

> JIM THE ENTERTAINER
> For Christ sake Shigoto. The woman is Stockholming you!

> SHIGOTO
> What?

> KATE
> What does that even mean?

> JIM THE ENTERTAINER
> She is Stockholm Syndroming you.
> You are befriending the victim.

> SHIGOTO
> Nonsense...

> KATE
> I'm glad we're establishing that
> I'm the victim here...

Jim gets right up in Shigoto's face in a demeaning manner.

> JIM THE ENTERTAINER
> She is playing with your head. Remember why
> she is here! Remember why she's the one tied to
> the chair! Every protest now it's just these jackasses like
> her showing up again and again, ruining our good work!
> And we need to get John so that we can –

> KATE
> Wait, good work? You're out there hurting and terrorizing
> "opinionated" civilians like *that's* the appropriate way to –

> JIM THE ENTERTAINER
> Kate, shut up!

An awkward beat.

> KATE
> Okay but I would just like to go on the record by stating
> that I was not intentionally Stockholming anyone.

> JIM THE ENTERTAINER
> Do you want to die, Kate?

                        KATE
        I don't feel a Thursday would be a particularly good day to.

He approaches her.

                  JIM THE ENTERTAINER
        Then why are you making it so painstakingly difficult
            for me to not put a bullet in your skull right now?

Kate doesn't break eye contact – she invites the threat.

                        KATE
            I thought I was here to be entertained. That title is
            very misleading. I mean, dude, the only time you've
            had me hooked was when I was on the floor.

Jim the Entertainer stares in her eyes... and laughs. A beat.

Violently, he whacks Kate across her face with the gun, sending her flying backwards in the chair. Her head hits the ground with incredible force.

Jim stands over her and aims. **BANG!** He fires a bullet into her leg. Kate screams in agony. She looks down to see blood rapidly pouring from her shin.

                        KATE
                      (in shock)
                    You... you shot me...

Disorientated, she quickly realizes she is facing away from the nail. In pain but determined, Kate chaotically reaches around with her tied hands trying to find it.

                  JIM THE ENTERTAINER
              (in the likeness of Maximus from 'Gladiator')
            'Are you not entertained? Are you not entertained?
                      Is this not why you are here?'

He drops the pose, chuckling cynically.

                  JIM THE ENTERTAINER
        You like that? Took that from *Gladiator*. Real old movie,
            you should check it out some time. Well, we'll see.

Jim walks over to a duffel bag full of supplies.

>   JIM THE ENTERTAINER
>   Shigoto, please.

Shigoto doesn't move. Confliction fills his eyes as he gazes at the bleeding Kate.

Tears stream down her face as she frantically reaches for the nail… getting closer and closer…

>   JIM THE ENTERTAINER
>   Shigoto!

Shigoto snaps out of it, grabbing the chair and lifting her up. Kate manages to grasp hold of the nail, pulling it free in the nick of time.

>   JIM THE ENTERTAINER
>   You want entertainment? I'll give you entertainment…
>   For our first act, I have prepared a game.

BANG! He fires a bullet into the air.

>   JIM THE ENTERTAINER *(cont'd)*
>   One in the Chamber.

>   KATE
>   *(softly)*
>   You're freaking crazy…

>   JIM THE ENTERTAINER
>   And your clock is ticking.

He stares at her as he opens the gun chamber, emptying all the bullets EXCEPT one (which is faintly seen). Kate watches them hit the floor. Spinning the chamber in, Jim points the gun to her head. Although in pain, she stares it down peculiarly unstirred…

>   JIM THE ENTERTAINER
>   We aren't that far from the nearest hospital,
>   you tell us what we want, we drop you off
>   and poof: all your troubles gone.

KATE
I'm happy to play your game, but shooting
me was quite uncalled for, wouldn't you say?

JIM THE ENTERTAINER
Damn... it might've been...
(shrugs)
No take backs now though.

CLOSE UP: of Kate's tied hands as she slowly files away at the rope with the nail.

KATE *(O.S.)*
Okay let's play your game. What do you want to know?

Jim paces.

JIM THE ENTERTAINER
It's gotten to the point where I think I might
actually believe you when you say you don't know
where he is. But what you do know is who does.

SHIGOTO
Just give us main associates, Kate.

KATE
That's what you want to know.

JIM THE ENTERTAINER
That's what we want to know, *right now*.

KATE
Okay.

She takes a deep breath of defeat.

KATE
There's seven of us in total. There's me,
there's John... there's Mike Litoris, my good
friend who you might know Jack Goff...

JIM THE ENTERTAINER
(unamused)
I see…

KATE
Who else…? Oh, Yu So Dum – he's
Vietnamese, very sweet man and –

Jim fires the gun – **BLANK**. No bullet. Kate doesn't even flinch. Strangely, she breaks out into an excited laughter.

KATE
I love this game! Let's go again.
Come on, ask me something else.
(breathes comically)
I'm ready.

CLOSE UP: of Kate's hands as the rope slowly tears.

SHIGOTO *(O.S.)*
Kate, you will bleed to death or get
shot if you no co-operate, please.

Jim stares on, frustrated.

JIM THE ENTERTAINER
I *really* don't think she understands the
severity of the situation she is in here.

KATE
(through her teeth)
No Entertainer Boy, I understand it just fine.

SHIGOTO
(nervously suggestive)
Kate you no answer, you may no live.

KATE
Yes I get it. So let's make this memorable then,
shall we? You got any more questions?

JIM THE ENTERTAINER	SHIGOTO
No.	Yes we –

ENANTIODROMIA

Immediately they both look to one another.

> SHIGOTO *(cont'd)*
> What you mean no?

> JIM THE ENTERTAINER
> *(suggestively)*
> *Follow my lead Shigoto.*

> SHIGOTO
> This is not plan –

> JIM THE ENTERTAINER
> Yeah and screw that, now I don't care anymore. I was nice enough to only shoot her in the leg the first time…

> KATE
> *(sotto)*
> Nice enough…?

> JIM THE ENTERTAINER
> … but clearly that didn't send the message. She's too stupid to see we mean business. So I'm going to shoot her in the head and find someone else that isn't *stubborn* and is willing to give us what we ask.

Shigoto yanks him away in a mini huddle.

> SHIGOTO
> *(increasingly angry)*
> She here now! To kidnap someone as simple would be difficult, no? Getting her was almost easy. It is only logical to question her. Maybe we put her on noose again, then she talk.

Kate nervously speeds up the tearing. Her face is draining of life as her wound continues to pour.

Jim stares at Shigoto with wide, suggestive eyes.

> JIM THE ENTERTAINER
> Shigoto, look at me. That hoe over there has no respect for us, and we're not going to get anywhere.

He pushes Shigoto off of him and re-approaches Kate, placing the gun against her temple.

              SHIGOTO
      I no sign up for this! Give me gun. Now!

Jim stares at Shigoto. He pulls the trigger – **BLANK**. No bullet. Once again Kate is bizarrely unfazed.

               KATE
    You're not playing by the rules Entertainer Boy.
    You're supposed to ask a question before you shoot.

Ignoring Kate, Jim continues to stare down the now furious Shigoto.

              SHIGOTO
             Give me gun.

          JIM THE ENTERTAINER
              (mockingly)
             Follow my plan.

Jim cocks the gun again.

              SHIGOTO
             (in Japanese)
        Screw your plan you imp!

          JIM THE ENTERTAINER
   Shigoto I can't understand you when you don't speak English!

              SHIGOTO
         You are foolish, stupid boy!

Kate tears vigorously behind her back.

          JIM THE ENTERTAINER
   Oh you're gonna insult me now, huh? What are you gonna
   do next, strap me to a chair and waterboard me too?

              SHIGOTO
     In Japan we have a word for people like you –

JIM THE ENTERTAINER
Yeah well I don't understand *that language* so I
could care less. Shigoto we have a job to do! Look
how unprofessional this is for her to see us…

He looks back at Kate - he then notices her arms moving rapidly behind her back.

SHIGOTO
(in Japanese)
I did not bring my family to this country for your stupidity!

JIM THE ENTERTAINER
(to Kate)
Wait a minute… What are you…

Shigoto lunges forward and grabs the gun, tussling with Jim. Kate watches in angst as she continues to tear.

JIM THE ENTERTAINER
What the hell are you doing man?!

Shigoto overpowers Jim and shoves him to the floor - pointing the gun at him.

SHIGOTO
You listen to me now?!

Jim the Entertainer lies there shaking his head in frustration.

JIM THE ENTERTAINER
Look at yourself Shigoto. You
let her Stockholm you man.

SUDDENLY – Kate breaks free from the chair and lunges forward, stabbing Shigoto in the hand with the nail. In the chaos, he pulls the trigger – **BLANK**, no bullet.

Shigoto yelps in pain as she rips the gun from him. Jim tries to get up but Kate quickly aims to him.

KATE
Don't move!

The men slowly put their hands up. Kate hobbles over to the duffel bag, blood still pouring from her leg. Her face is now drained of life.

> JIM THE ENTERTAINER
> *(nervously laughing)*
> Kate. Okay, listen you don't have to shoot anyone of us.
> We can figure something out here. Kate...?

> KATE
> Oh shut up.

Kate holds the gun to her head and cocks it.

> JIM THE ENTERTAINER
> Woah, woah, woah...!

She clicks the trigger – **BLANK**. No bullet. Jim the Entertainer and Shigoto are left perplexed.

> KATE
> I know you emptied the gun, idiot.

Jim is even more confused. Kate winces as she bends down and picks up the cartridge of bullets.

> KATE *(cont'd)*
> *(weakly)*
> But I got the bullets now, *hoe*, and I'm going to
> walk out those doors. If either of you takes one
> step I will load this and shoot you both.

The two men nervously stay still. Kate slowly backs up before turning and limping towards the door. A beat.

Kate collapses to the floor, passing out. The gun and bullets scatter across the ground. No movement.

The two men look to one another. They drop their hands and cautiously move towards her. Kate is out cold.

> JIM THE ENTERTAINER
> *(whispering)*
> Keep an eye on her Shigoto.

Jim moves and grabs the gun, picking up a handful of bullets that lie around it. He looks down the barrel.

                    JIM THE ENTERTAINER
                     I could've sworn I left one…

Aiming towards the floor he fires – **BLANK**. No bullet.

Kate JOLTS to life. She rapidly looks around visibly disorientated.

                    JIM THE ENTERTAINER
          Kate. You really got damn close there! You had me in
          the first half, not gonna lie. I thought we were finished.

He waves around the pistol tauntingly.

                    JIM THE ENTERTAINER
                          (cynically)
                    But now I got the gun.

Kate is visibly defeated. Jim the Entertainer let's loose a devilish smile, while continuing to gesture with the weapon.

                    JIM THE ENTERTAINER
      Did you really think you were going to get out of here
      when there's two of us and one of you though? That was
          your first mistake. I mean you talk about being logical
         but do you know how easy it's going to be for –

BANG! The pistol goes off and shoots Shigoto in his knee. Shigoto lets out a wailing scream. Kate jumps.

                            SHIGOTO
                        (in Japanese)
                  You shot me! You bastard –

                    JIM THE ENTERTAINER
           Oh my God, Shigoto bro I'm sorry!
      Calm down alright, you need to apply pressure…

Kate is stunned – realizing she could have killed herself.

                    SHIGOTO
            Screw you! My wife is going to kill me!

Kate crawls backwards until knocking into the exit door. Quickly she pulls herself up and limps out the warehouse.

                JIM THE ENTERTAINER *(O.S.)*
                        (fading)
        I'm so sorry man... You're really bleeding dude. Like a lot...

INT. HALLWAYS, WAREHOUSE – CONTINUOUS

Kate frantically limps through the dimly lit corridors. Behind her, Shigoto screams echo throughout.

Down one hallway she spots a fire escape. She rapidly hobbles towards it bursting through...

EXT. HILL TOP – DAY; CONTINUOUS

... and out of the building. Kate catches her breath.

                    DIOMEDES *(O.S.)*
                Damn girl, you a mess.

She looks up – a teenaged black male stands before her, smoking a cigarette. This is DIOMEDES. Behind him is an open MOVING TRUCK with a large rectangular box inside it. He takes one last hit before stomping the cigarette out.

                    DIOMEDES
                Sorry about this.

Diomedes punches her in the face.

                                        CUT TO BLACK

FADE IN ON…

INT. WAREHOUSE – DAY

Faint voices argue as Kate slowly awakens. In pain she tries to reach for her head - her whole body is tightly restrained to the chair once more.

Shigoto stands supported by a stick – his knee bandaged and bloody. Jim aims the gun at Kate. <u>Masks are now off</u>.

> JIM THE ENTERTAINER
> Well, well, well Kate. Here we are again. Face to face.

She looks down to her leg, it is now bandaged but soaked.

> JIM THE ENTERTAINER
> We've agreed that you've caused us too much trouble for us to *ever* let you out alive here now. But we figured we wanted you to live to see our final act. One last F.U. to the A.A.F.'s.

> KATE
> *(exhaustedly)*
> I told you, I'm not gonna talk –

> JIM THE ENTERTAINER
> Yeah, yeah we don't care about that anymore Kate. The whole question game is so played out and boring. So how's about we skip to the finale with a twist, huh?

He hands Shigoto the gun as he approaches her, leaning close to her ear.

> JIM THE ENTERTAINER
> And you'll never see it coming.

Rapidly he pulls a knife and cuts her hands and feet loose.

> JIM THE ENTERTAINER
> Behind you is a pretty cool homie named Diomedes.

As she stands, she turns to see Diomedes leaning against the large rectangular box. He nods.

                    DIOMEDES
                      Sup.

                JIM THE ENTERTAINER
      You may recognize him as the Anti-Fascist that kidnapped
         you and brought you to us. And miraculously, Diomedes
       has found the answer to our troubles this whole time. A solution
            rather. Tell her what you have inside that package there bro.

                    DIOMEDES
           I nabbed your boy John Witherspoon.
            Beat his ass and shot him in the dome.

Kate's heart sinks at the words.

                      KATE
                I don't believe you.

         SHIGOTO   JIM THE ENTERTAINER
       (voice pained)   *(quickly after)*
     We figure you say that —   We knew you would say that
                                       Kate. Show her Shigoto.

Shigoto tosses polaroids onto the floor. Shaking, Kate slowly drops on her
knees picking up the pictures. In them: John is beat up, bloody, and DEAD.

Tears begin to form in her eyes.

                      KATE
                  You're liars.

                JIM THE ENTERTAINER
          I have been many things to you today
          Kate, but a liar is not one of them.

He motions to Diomedes who wheels the box over to Kate, slamming it
down. Jim hands Diomedes some cash.

              JIM THE ENTERTAINER *(O.S.)*
          Now... there's one last request we have
              of you Kate. Before we off you.

He drops the knife at her feet.

> JIM THE ENTERTAINER
> You are going to cut open that box, and see him for yourself;
> what all this Anti-Anti nonsense and stupidity has brought
> us to! And then, you're going to free his head for us.

> KATE
> Do you hear yourself? You're insane.

> JIM THE ENTERTAINER
> Do it.

He grabs the gun from Shigoto and cocks it, resting it on Kate's skull. She doesn't move.

> JIM THE ENTERTAINER *(cont'd)*
> *(screaming)*
> Do it!

Kate breaks into tears. She grabs the knife and stabs the box. Fearfully she begins to cut around the edges.

> JIM THE ENTERTAINER
> Hurry up!

Kate rips open the box. Inside is a VINTAGE REFRIGERATOR.

> JIM THE ENTERTAINER
> This is it Kate. Show's over. Open it.

Kate looks down at the photos and cries harder.

> JIM THE ENTERTAINER
> Kate! Open it now!

Kate lifts the lid of the refrigerator. She leans over and looks inside.

SUDDENLY – she drops to the floor. An arm reaches out with a gun. **BANG! BANG!** Jim the Entertainer and Shigoto collapse on the ground – IMMEDIATELY DEAD.

Kate breathes heavily, the room falls otherwise silent. From out of the box, the professionally-dressed JOHN WITHERSPOON emerges, alive and well.

He looks at the two dead bodies and lowers his gun.

> JOHN
> Help me out.

Kate struggles to help pull him up. He walks over to and examines the bodies.

> JOHN
> You okay?

No answer. He turns to Kate, she is completely pale.

> JOHN
> Kate.

She collapses.

> JOHN
> *(beat)*
> Kate.

No response. He calmly approaches her and checks her pulse.

> JOHN
> Dio.

Diomedes is lent up against a wall, smoking a cigarette.

> DIOMEDES
> Sup cuz.

> JOHN
> Call up Luis for me.

Diomedes pulls out a burner phone and starts dialing. John examines Kate's injuries – the bruises on her face.

> JOHN
> You really had to hit her this hard?

                    DIOMEDES
        You told me to make it believable. I apologized.

Diomedes walks over next to John with the phone pressed to his ear. Both looming over the Anti-Fascist corpses. John hands him a handful of pristine $50 bills. Diomedes counts.

                    DIOMEDES
                Whatchu you wanna do?

                      JOHN
           Trash 'em. Make them disappear. We got one
           more delivery for the day then you're through.

                    DIOMEDES
                      Dope.
                    (into phone)
                    Ayo Louie…

Diomedes walks towards the warehouse doors as he explains the situation over the phone.

John looks down at Kate and the scene one last time. There is a slight discomfort in his eyes, as if he promised something that couldn't be fulfilled. He brushes it off.

                      JOHN
                Alright. Let's go to work.

              OPERATING SYSTEM *(V.O.)*
            'Going To Work': resuming playlist.

[MUSIC CUE: "PIANO CONCERTO NO.2 IN C MINOR, OP.18: II. ADAGIO SOSTENUTO - SONG RESUMES]

John looks up to the source of music as the classical song fills the blood covered room.

INT. WAREHOUSE OFFICE – DUSK

CLOSE UP: on the old TV screen. The WLT news logo finishes.

THE LEVER DU CINÉ COLLECTION : RENAISSANCE

> NEWS ANCHOR JANET
> Good evening Los Angeles this is Janet from Channel 24 WLT News, with the 6pm Broadcast. The riots in Downtown L.A. continue to escalate, as police struggle to gain control of the rapidly growing conflict.

EXT. HILL TOP – DUSK

Diomedes pulls out a massive folded box and two body bags from the back of the moving truck.

As he does so, a 2000s Nissan pulls up to the top of the hill, parking next to him. LUIS (mid30s, Hispanic) and HANNAH (early 20s) exit the vehicle.

> NEWS ANCHOR JANET *(V.O.)*
> What originally started as a highly anticipated campaign event quickly spiraled into the historic political street battle that is still now unfolding, when Antifa extremists arrived to the scene and began to violently attack the Fascist ralliers. Short afterwards, the Anti-Anti-Fascists too arrived to the scene; dishing out to Antifa what they too had served. Just to clarify for all viewers now tuning in…

INT. WAREHOUSE – DUSK

Luis and Hannah enter the warehouse, greeted by John. Luis goes to check Kate's pulse. Hannah watches anxiously as he carries her out the room.

Diomedes zips up the two dead bodies into separate bags. John builds the new box as Hannah hoses the room. John places the nail back in the EXACT SPOT that it was taken.

> NEWS ANCHOR JANET *(V.O.)*
> John Witherspoon, the leader of the A.A.F. movement, is still missing at this point in time, with no current leads to his whereabouts, although the police still suspect Antifa to be involved. When we have more to report on the situation we will inform you here first. However at this time, we advise everyone to stay indoors as Downtown Los Angeles continues to burn during this historic period of political unrest…

John climbs into the refrigerator and lies down. Hannah hands him a loaded gun as she closes the lid shut.

EXT. WAREHOUSE, HILL TOP – DUSK

The Nissan is now gone. Hannah and Diomedes (on the phone) lift the box upright into the back of the truck before placing the two corpses inside.

> JOHN *(V.O.)*
> *(through phone)*
> Once you dump them, take the truck down the 2 until you reach the city, back roads only from there on out.

> DIOMEDES
> Yeah I got it cuz.

> HANNAH
> Come help me please.

Diomedes ties Hannah's hands behind her back.

> JOHN *(V.O.)*
> You know the A.F. types to look for.
> Tell them the plan and get them to bite the bait.

Hannah climbs into the back of the truck. Diomedes pulls out a bag and places it over her head.

> JOHN *(V.O.)*
> Also: drive carefully please.

> DIOMEDES
> Yeah, whatever g.

He shuts the doors.

EXT. HILL TOP – CONTINUOUS

The truck drives down the hill, away from the warehouse.

INT. BACK OF TRUCK – CONTINUOUS

The bagged Hannah sits next to the box.

> HANNAH
> Enantiodromia... Enantiodromia...
> Enantiodromia... Enantiodromia...

EXT. LOS ANGELES – DUSK

[PIANO CONCERTO REACHES CLIMATIC END]

SERIES OF SHOTS: of peaceful suburban Los Angeles as the sun sets on the city, each turning darker and more chaotic as they get closer to the heart of the downtown riots.

Then, the view from the warehouse hill of the smoke covered Los Angeles, as the sun sets, and composition concludes.

> FADE TO BLACK
>
> ROLL CREDITS
>
> THE END

The Wine Glass (between 1658-1660) by Johannes Vermeer (1632-1675)

There Was a Knock at the Door 1 2 3

Written by

Lever du Ciné

SUPERIMPOSE TITLE: **There Was a Knock at the Door 1 2 3**

BANG BANG BANG. The instantaneous sound of knocking on a door.

CUT IN ON

EXT. LOS ANGELES SUBURBAN APARTMENT – DUSK

A front door swings open – a man (late 20s, a bit nerdy looking) stands in the doorway dressed in nice dinner date attire. This is RALPHIE. He has on soapy kitchen gloves.

> RALPHIE
> Hey.

A pretty Latina woman (late 20s, a New Yorker born and breed) stands in front of him in a slim fit dress. This is MARGARITA.

> MARGARITA
> Hey.

> RALPHIE
> You look fine.

> MARGARITA
> *(smiles)*
> Thanks.

> RALPHIE
> Not fine as in okay, fine as in bad.

They stare at each other for a brief moment.

> RALPHIE *(cont'd)*
> Not bad as in naughty, bad as in –

> MARGARITA
> You um... you gonna invite me in or like... what's good?

> RALPHIE
> Oh yeah come in please, sorry.

He stands aside as she enters in.

INT. LOS ANGELES SUBURBAN APARTMENT – CONTINUOUS

Ralphie and Margarita enter the living room. The dining table is moved into the center of the room, and a full meal awaits. Classic 1930s music sets the mood.

> RALPHIE
> Welcome to my humble abode.

> MARGARITA
> Not bad. You always keep your dining table in the middle of the living room?

> RALPHIE
> Yeah it's kinda crammed in the kitchen so I do this when I have hot dates over.

> MARGARITA
> So just this once.

> RALPHIE
> Yeah this is pretty much the first time. If you want to sit and get comfortable, I'm just gonna finish washing the dishes and then we can dig in.

> MARGARITA
> Bet.

Ralphie goes into the kitchen. Margarita walks around his apartment examining all the displays: antiques, posters, paintings...

> MARGARITA
> You paint?

> RALPHIE (O.S.)
> Nah that's my roommate's girlfriend's work. You like?

> MARGARITA
> Yeah they're pretty neat.

Margarita stares at a YOUTUBE PLAQUE on the wall – **100k subscribers for Wreck-It Ralphie Reviews.**

> RALPHIE *(O.S.)*
> She's a pretty big-time artist out here, she does galleries all over the country, I feel like you two would really hit it off.

> MARGARITA
> Cool.

> RALPHIE *(O.S.)*
> I'm really glad you came Margarita. Not gonna lie I was kinda nervous that you wouldn't show.

> MARGARITA
> Why is that?

As she continues browsing, a bizarre but stunning GLASS PORCUPINE housed in a case catches her eye.

> RALPHIE *(O.S.)*
> I wasn't sure how into me you were.

> MARGARITA
> I gave you my number, didn't I? *You* were the one that waited to text me like two days afterwards, so…

INT. KITCHEN – CONTINUOUS

Ralphie scrubs hard on a dish.

> RALPHIE
> Yeah well I was spending that time trying to decide whether or not I believed the number you gave me was real or scam likely.

> MARGARITA *(O.S.)*
> You sound paranoid.

> RALPHIE
> I mean you know how dating is nowadays.
> Also... I've admittedly never flirted with one
> of you before so I didn't know if I was getting
> played or not, you know? It's really hard to tell –

Margarita now stands at the kitchen entrance.

> MARGARITA
> *'One of me'*? The hell's that supposed to mean?

> RALPHIE
> Sorry I didn't mean it like that, I... what I was trying to say –

> MARGARITA
> What were you just trying to say, *Ralphie*?

> RALPHIE
> New Yorker. I've never had a date with a girl from New York.

> MARGARITA
> And?

> RALPHIE
> *And*... and well... you... you girls kinda intimidate me...

She stares at him for a beat.

> MARGARITA
> You moron.

> RALPHIE
> What?

> MARGARITA
> That's how you wash your dishes?

The dishes sit in a pool of dirty soap water.

> RALPHIE
> What? What about it?

MARGARITA
Nah that's real gross dude. You nasty.

RALPHIE
What are you talking about, this is
the normal way to wash dishes —

MARGARITA
No, it really is not.

RALPHIE
Every human being I've ever known washes their dishes
just like this. It's like a bath for the dishes. You scrub
them, and then you put them in the soapy water and let
them bathe a little, ya know what I'm saying?

MARGARITA
First off, no I do not know what you're saying, no I
don't relate, because that is *gross*. Second, I'm starting to
suspect that you're a grown man that also still takes baths?

He shrugs.

MARGARITA
(sarcastically)
That's not a red flag.

RALPHIE
Okay maybe you're still stuck in the New York way of
doing things Margarita, but here in L.A. we wash dishes
like this, and grown men relish bathing. Baths are
extremely relieving and sacred... and sexy, okay?

MARGARITA
(not buying it)
Mhm. Okay.

RALPHIE
Alright forget the dishes, I didn't spend four hours
attempting to prepare a gourmet meal just for you
to violate my dishwashing skills. *Dish washing?*

MARGARITA
Okay Gordon Ramsey lets eat then, I'm hungry anyway.

RALPHIE
Thank you.

MARGARITA
(slick whisper)
You and your purple gloves...

Ralphie turns and flicks water at her.

RALPHIE
Aht. Aht. Go sit.

MARGARITA
Alright chill, damn.

INT. LIVING ROOM – MOMENTS LATER

Ralphie lifts the lids on the food: salmon, vegetables, pasta in sauce. Pre-made margaritas compliment the meal.

RALPHIE
A hunch told me you like pasta so you know I had
to pull up the best recipe a homie could find.

He looks to her, hoping for approval.

MARGARITA
I do enjoy pasta.

RALPHIE
Well then I'm just a man on top of my game then sheesh.

MARGARITA
Yeah we'll see. It's not the pasta I'm worried about though dude.

RALPHIE
Worried? What are you worried about?

She picks up a plate.

                    MARGARITA
        Did you give these plates a bath too or —

                     RALPHIE
        Alright, alright I get it I'm gross, can we eat.

                    MARGARITA
            I just wanted to prove my point. But
           fine, it looks good, I wanna eat, let's eat.

She takes a seat. He picks up a bottle of champagne and begins uncorking it.

                     RALPHIE
     Damn. I have a feeling you're gonna be nothing but trouble.

Ralphie pulls and pulls…

POP! The champagne bottle opens.

INT. LIVING ROOM – MOMENTS LATER

The two eat from their plates. Classic 1930s music continues to play.

                     RALPHIE
         How have you not even seen a whale before like…
              like, that doesn't make any sense to me —

                    MARGARITA
          I don't know what you want me to tell you guy,
           not everyone had Sea World right around the
            corner when they were growing up like you did.

                     RALPHIE
       Forget Sea World, you lived in New York City and
           you've never gone Whale Watching before?

                    MARGARITA
                    Whale Watching?

RALPHIE
Whale Watching. I feel like that's such a New York thing,
New Yorkers have been Whale Watching. You're a New Yorker
so logically you've had to have gone Whale Watching.

MARGARITA
Boy that has to be the whitest thing I've ever heard of.

RALPHIE
I mean I've never gone Whale Watching, I've just seen
whales out by the pier etc., but like... I can't imagine never
having seen the largest mammal before *ever* in my life.

MARGARITA
Why is this so important?

RALPHIE
That you've been Whale Watching?

MARGARITA
That I've seen a whale?

RALPHIE
Well because...
(beat)
I don't even remember how we got
here from the original conversation...

MARGARITA
You were talking all about that guy in the club
that was hitting on me first before you made you're
approach, and you compared his appetite...

| **MARGARITA** | **RALPHIE** |
| ... to a whale. | ... Appetite to a whale, yeah! |

MARGARITA
Yes, because he just kept ordering
bottom-less appetizers at the club and devouring
them in like one bite each or whatever.

RALPHIE
How unhinged do you have to be to
order appetizers at a night club...?

MARGARITA
And then I said 'whales are goofy creatures when you think
about it right?', and I started talking about how I couldn't imagine
being by one, and then for the last seven-eight minutes you've
just been clowning me for never having seen a whale...?

RALPHIE
I mean I stand by my clownery. It's baffling to
me that you haven't seen one of them.

MARGARITA
Regardless of how you feel, who cares about
seeing the largest mammal though? I've seen them
thick blue blobs dozens of times on the Discovery Channel,
Animal Planet... like does it make anyone less of a
person because they ain't never seen a whale, in person?

RALPHIE
I mean I don't know, it just feels like a prerequisite
of existence. Maybe it's just that women don't...

She shoots him a fighting look. He catches himself.

RALPHIE *(cont'd)*
… You haven't told me what you thought about the food.
What do you think about the food Margarita?

MARGARITA
It's good. Can't complain.

He gives her a glance, wanting more.

MARGARITA
I like it. Never thought to try champagne-drenched
Salmon before, I'll give you that.

                    RALPHIE
That's what I've been saying, it's killer right!
My little signature touch. And I got you with them
little margaritas on the side, specially crafted for
a beautiful girl named Margarita, ya feel me?

                    MARGARITA
                    (reservedly)
            It is also very good.

They continue to eat.

                    RALPHIE
    Did your parents like, really like margaritas or —

                    MARGARITA
        I should probably tell you now that
            my name isn't really Margarita.

Ralphie stops eating, confused.

                    VALENTINA
        My name is Valentina. I told you my
        name was Margarita at the club so you —

                    RALPHIE
            So I would buy you margaritas...

A beat. He laughs.

                    RALPHIE
        Genius. I really spent near 100 bucks
            on margaritas alone that night.

                    VALENTINA
            You don't sound upset.

                    RALPHIE
        I mean.... I respect the hustle...?
                    (beat)
            Plus, shoot, I guess it still
            kinda got you here, didn't it?

                        VALENTINA
                        I guess it did.

He raises his glass.

                        RALPHIE
                   To Valentina Margarita then.

She shrugs.

                        VALENTINA
                     Valentina Margarita.

CLINK! Their glasses collide together.

INT. KITCHEN – MOMENTS LATER

A tequila bottle on the kitchen counter is low in fluids. Multiple squeezed limes lie beside it.

Loud laughter seeps from the other room.

INT. LIVING ROOM – CONTINUOUS

Valentina and Ralphie have finished their food, but alcohol is still flowing. Ralphie is standing, deep into story.

                        RALPHIE
                 … I had already lost my patience with
                 this crackhead but he was damn relentless!

                        VALENTINA
                     Relentless you say.

                        RALPHIE
              Absolutely *relentless*! Like there was no getting
                past him. He's standing in front of me hitting
              the meanest break dance I've ever seen. *The meanest*
                 Margarita, like – I mean Valentina, he was like –

He dances like a madman for Valentina. She dies of laughter.

RALPHIE
Poppin' lockin' droppin', the whole shebang.
Meanwhile, dozens of people are passing right by,
Walking on past him... but every time I try to go around –

He demonstrates again, more into it. She laughs even harder.

VALENTINA
Why though?

RALPHIE
I still have no clue Valentina!

VALENTINA
So what did you do?

RALPHIE
My roommate Juan is behind him at this point because
of course he let's that jackass by, no conflict. So I'm
looking to him with the most earnest plea for help in
my eyes. Like if my eyes could speak, they were screaming,
I was begging. So after Juan is finally done laughing
and it's getting to the point where he's actually concerned
for my safety if I don't participate in this crackhead's
dance battle, he comes up with this... *'bright idea'*.

VALENTINA
Oh God, I'm not ready.

RALPHIE
One stupid idea. He taps this psychopath on the shoulder
and shouts: "Watch out! He's got a knife! He's got a knife!"

VALENTINA
What.

RALPHIE
Juan put a death sentence on me. I kid you not,
this dude's eyes open anime wide, and he was after me
like the FDA to a tax evader. He was hell bent, he was –

VALENTINA
The IRS you mean.

> RALPHIE
> Can I finish?

> VALENTINA
> Yeah but with more accurate analogies please.

> RALPHIE
> Forget the metaphor woman, this man had
> murder in his eyes dammit! It went from 0-100 like
> *that* – a dance battle to kill or be killed. Now I think
> I could hold my own in a fight right...

She unsurely gestures "50-50".

> RALPHIE *(cont'd)*
> ... but when you see an 120 something pound
> Crackhead running at you, all the fight in your DNA
> just *pft*... out of the precipice of your being.

> VALENTINA
> So you ran.

> RALPHIE
> I turned and bolted like a little boy I am not even
> ashamed to admit it. I ran so hard, I ran for what
> felt like nine city blocks without stopping, without
> looking back not once. I crossed through traffic I-I,
> I knocked over pedestrians. And I got to a point where
> I was like: alright I'm out of breath, I can't run anymore,
> I think I pulled my hamstring two blocks back, and now
> I gotta have a final stand, you know? So I look back and –

BANG BANG BANG. There is a knock at the door. Both turn to look.

> VALENTINA
> Who is that?

> RALPHIE
> I don't know...

He walks to the door, looking through the peep hole.

> JUAN *(O.S.)*
> Ralphie open up man I forgot my suit! Quick bro!

RALPHIE
What's the magic word?

VALENTINA
Who is that?

JUAN *(O.S.)*
Bro my ass is late for Scarlett's gallery,
and I'ma tell her it was your dumbass too
so she'll cuss you out again. Hurry up.

RALPHIE
So toxic man.
(to Valentina)
It's just Juan.

Ralphie opens the door. His slick haired, Hispanic roommate quickly enters in, stripping out of a construction uniform as he works his way through the living room.

RALPHIE
You forgot your suit?

JUAN
Yeah bro, I woke up late and left without it, and
she's been gallery stressed all week long, *and on top of
that* it's her monthly so I'm living right now dangerous g.
(to Valentina)
Hey how's it going.

RALPHIE
Valentina, you may remember my
roommate Juan from the other night.

VALENTINA
Yeah I do, hi.

JUAN
Valentina? Wasn't your name Margarita?

RALPHIE
There's a long story to —

VALENTINA
I told him my name was Margarita
so he'd buy me more margaritas.

JUAN
Genius.
(to Ralphie)
You're an idiot.

RALPHIE
Don't you need to get that suit?

Juan swiftly disappears into a hall. They sit silently.

RALPHIE
(calling out)
You changing here too bro?

Juan returns with a clean suit in wrap.

JUAN
Nah no time. Alright I'm out of your hair.
(to Valentina)
Nice seeing you again.

VALENTINA
Yeah you too.

Juan looks at Ralphie suggestively, Ralphie pushes him towards the door. Juan exits out, Ralphie locks it.

RALPHIE
You ready for dessert?

VALENTINA
Oh yes please. Finish the story though, what happened?

Ralphie goes into the kitchen.

RALPHIE *(O.S.)*
What part did I leave off at?

Valentina looks back at the GLASS PORCUPINE.

VALENTINA
You ran nine blocks or whatever, dodging traffic,
and then you finally look back and…?

Ralphie returns with a cheesecake.

RALPHIE
I look back and nothing. No crackhead to be found. He had
to have given up somewhere between those nine blocks but
I'll never know for sure. So long story short, that is why I'll never
step foot within that entire radius of Hollywood Blvd again.

VALENTINA
Wow.

RALPHIE
I know. Okay Madame, to conclude this romantic
dinner date, I present to thee: New York style cheesecake.

VALENTINA
Why was your choice in romantic
dinner date dessert, cheesecake?

RALPHIE
(as if common sense)
Because you're New Yorken.
All New Yorkers love cheesecake.

VALENTINA
'New Yorken' is probably the most stupidest thing
I've ever heard come out of someone's lips.

RALPHIE
How?

VALENTINA
That's not even a real term dummy you just made that up.

RALPHIE
I pretty sure that's a real thing.

VALENTINA
Also why do you keep saying that?

RALPHIE
Why do I keep saying what?

VALENTINA
'All New Yorkers do this', 'all New Yorkers love that'.
Do you think that's like our one personality trait or something?
Being a New Yorker? Like that's the one archetype for *all*
New Yorkers, we *all* love and do the same things.

RALPHIE
Look alright I'm sorry, I just… you didn't give me a lot
to go off of. When I asked you what you liked to eat you
said 'surprise me'. When I asked you what you like to do
you said 'anything simple'. So I googled 'what do
New Yorkers like'. That's all the subject material I had,
I had so little to work with here Valentina Margarita.

VALENTINA
Well stereotypes are a bit of a lousy attempt if you ask me.

RALPHIE
We can go out and get ice cream… or cake, we can go
get some cake if that's what you'd prefer, yeah?

Valentina sticks her fork into the cheesecake and begins eating.

VALENTINA
Nah I freaking love cheesecake don't worry about it.

RALPHIE
Then why the hell were you giving
me such a hard time about it!

VALENTINA
Because I hate that you planned a whole date
revolving around 'New Yorken' stereotypes and
you just happened to get lucky with all them.

RALPHIE
Valentina. Don't hate the player…

He smirks as he takes a bite of the cheesecake.

RALPHIE *(cont'd)*
… hate the game baby.

VALENTINA
Cringe. What's the deal with the glass porcupine.

RALPHIE
What?

VALENTINA
The glass porcupine behind me.

RALPHIE
Oh. My mother gave me that before I moved out here.

VALENTINA
Does it have any meaning?

RALPHIE
Eh, just some old family heirloom. It's something that her father gave to her. He wanted a son but she was the only child he got so he passed it down to her. His father gave it to him, and so on. Supposedly it belonged to some royalty that was living in the colonies during the settling times or whatever.

VALENTINA
And you just keep it out in the open like that?

RALPHIE
Where else would I keep it? In a box in the attic?

She shrugs.

VALENTINA
Why'd you move to L.A.?

RALPHIE
I'm a dreamer baby. Come on now.

VALENTINA
Isn't everyone these days.

RALPHIE
Yeah... and basically everyone's got
one of those around here too.

He lazily gestures to his YouTube plaque. They eat silently for a moment.

RALPHIE
Me leaving was hard on my mom.

VALENTINA
What about you?

RALPHIE
Me as well but harder for her. Since I was five all we
really had was each other, and as much as I'd like to see her
all the time, I don't really have the time because, well... life.
When I left, she gave me that thing to show how much
I mean to her, but I already know how much I mean to
her so basically she just gave me more responsibility.

He chuckles. Valentina studies him for moment.

VALENTINA
Seems like a great mom.

RALPHIE
Yeah she's alright.
(beat)
What about you?

VALENTINA
What about me?

RALPHIE
Why'd you give up the glamorous New Yorken lifestyle
to move all the way out to this City of Traffic?

VALENTINA
(slight chuckle)
The life I lived over there was *far* from glamorous my guy.

> RALPHIE
> Okay but I'm sure you had a bunch of rich old hedge funders vying for you over there. No?

> VALENTINA
> Shoot. I actually really did.

> RALPHIE
> So? Why'd you leave then?

She zones for a second, playing with her fork.

> VALENTINA
> My apartment got broken into. While I was in it.

> RALPHIE
> Oh damn, what... that's terrifying.

> VALENTINA
> Yeah.

> RALPHIE
> How did it happen if you don't mind me...?

> VALENTINA
> Nah, it's fine. Three guys entered my apartment one night. One of them held me at gunpoint, while the other two completely stripped my apartment.

> RALPHIE
> Jesus...

> VALENTINA
> *Completely stripped*. I'm talking Grinch-type stripping – nothing left except my bed.

> RALPHIE
> Bastards. That's horrible Valentina. They didn't... they didn't do any –

> VALENTINA
> Nah. No.

RALPHIE
I can't imagine having gone through something like that.

A beat.

VALENTINA
Okay this is honestly some damn good cheesecake.

RALPHIE
Right?

VALENTINA
Where did you get this from?

RALPHIE
Come on now, I can't tell you that.

VALENTINA
Oh come on, please. Please…!

RALPHIE
Uh-uh. We gatekeep around here.
You gotta come back if you want more.

VALENTINA
You drive a hard bargain.

RALPHIE
Only because I think I might like you Valentina.

VALENTINA
I might like you too. Ralphie.

They share a smile.

RALPHIE
But wait – go back just a second and explain to me
this real quick: so you move out here because your house
got broken into, but like, L.A. is literally notorious for
being as dangerous as or maybe even more so –

                    VALENTINA
            Yeah sorry, I didn't explain myself well
            enough. I came out here *to rob* houses.

Ralphie pauses. He humorously eyes her up. Finally, she breaks a smile, triggering laughter from both.

                    VALENTINA
            I'm messing with you, I moved out
            here because I fell in love.

                    RALPHIE
            Oh. Okay. Well sorry for the guy it didn't work
            out for. One's man's trash, is another man's
            come up. Am I right? Can we drink to that?

                    VALENTINA
            Okay Macklemore, 2012 called.

He pours more for both.

                    RALPHIE
            Well, what happened between you two?

                    VALENTINA
            What do you mean?

                    RALPHIE
            Like why did it end?

                    VALENTINA
            You're noisy!

                    RALPHIE
            Eh… just curious.

Valentina takes out her phone and sends a text.

                    VALENTINA
            To answer that dude, you'd have to know how it
            started and, well that's a whole other long, and boring –

                     RALPHIE
                I got time Valentina.

She locks eyes with him.

                     RALPHIE *(cont'd)*
                 How did it start?

Valentina takes a deep breath. A beat.

                    VALENTINA
              There was a knock at the door.

BANG BANG BANG! Immediately there is a hard knock at the door.

Ralphie turns to look, but Valentina stays focused on him. He laughs.

                     RALPHIE
            Yo that is some unreal timing! What!
            That made me jump a little not gonna lie. Man
            that clown Juan must've forgot something else.

He goes to get up.

                     RALPHIE
              Wait until he hears about –

                    VALENTINA
                      Not yet.

Ralphie pauses.

                    VALENTINA
            I didn't finish telling you my story.

                     RALPHIE
                     Yeah but…

                    VALENTINA
         See, there was a knock at the door, I opened it.
         Three men entered in. One holds me at gun point,
         the other two robbed me of everything I have, right?

VALENTINA *(cont'd)*
While that's all going on, as I starred – weak and powerless – into the eyes of the asshole who stood before me, for one second, out of no where… I felt something. Not fear, I wasn't scared or anything… but… I felt, this strange feeling of lust…? Desire? The power in those ferocious hazel eyes was almost alluring to me –

RALPHIE *(O.S.)*
Valentina…?

VALENTINA
It was *entrancing*, that's the word. It was one of those moments where you both connected to that same undeniable feeling. You know?

RALPHIE *(O.S.)*
Valentina maybe I should…

VALENTINA
And after they had taken everything, stripped me of all my physical possessions and what not, he looked me in my eyes one last time and the most peculiar thing left his lips. He looked at me and said: *'We weren't born stars, but we can still reach them.'*

RALPHIE *(O.S.)*
Valentina… Maybe I should answer the door –

VALENTINA
Not. Yet. That's what he said to me. He told me that, and something finally clicked. It was as if those words unlocked something in my wiring, in my being, and just like that I walked out the door right then and there with them. Never returned to that apartment again, never looked back.

Beat. Ralphie stares at her uneased.

                    VALENTINA
As I told you, I came here for love. But not for
the love of some man. Maybe at first that's what I
thought it was, but I realized at one point it wasn't him
that I was drawn to, no. No... I knew from the first second
I actually took part in it that all he was to me was just
the awakening. Instead it was for that *feeling*. That *power*.
Having all the cards in my hands, the dramatic irony of the
game; nothing beats that feeling. No thing, no man. *Nothing*.

                    RALPHIE *(O.S.)*
            Valentina, you're kinda scaring me.

Intensity continues to burn on her face… and then, a calm warm smile.

                    VALENTINA
            Ralphie, gosh I'm only kidding.

                    RALPHIE
        Yo. You've got the darkest sense of humor I have
        ever seen. It was kinda sexy though, you really were
        committed to that whole sphiel for a second there.

Beat.

                    RALPHIE *(cont'd)*
    Spiel…? Sphill… did I say that right at least once?

                    VALENTINA
                It's spiel, dude.

She looks at the time on her phone.

                    VALENTINA *(cont'd)*
                    It's spiel.
                    (beat)
                Good boy, good fun.

THUD! The front door is kicked in.

EXT. LOS ANGELES SUBURBAN APARTMENT – NIGHT; CONTINUOUS

Visible from outside the apartment living room window, three men burst in. one hits Ralphie hard on his head, and tosses Valentina a gun. She stands and watches Ralphie as the rest inaudibly ransack his apartment. After a moment, one of the men quickly shuts the blinds.

TIMECUT:

EXT. LOS ANGELES SUBURBAN APARTMENT – NIGHT

Red and blue lights flash outside of the now taped off apartment. The blinds are gone.

INT. LOS ANGELES SUBURBAN APARTMENT – CONTINUOUS

Police continue to scour the barren apartment for evidence. Ralphie sits lent up against a wall, icing his head.

Juan talks to the police, glancing over at Ralphie in a disappointed frustration.

>OFFICER MATTHEWS *(O.S.)*
>Randolph Bronti.

A female officer approaches him.

>RALPHIE
>Just Ralphie ma'am...

>OFFICER MATTHEWS *(O.S.)*
>You've reported to Officer Nichols that everything was taken, correct?

>RALPHIE
>*(unfocused)*
>Yeah. Everything's gone, she... they took...

OFFICER MATTHEWS *(O.S.)*
We found something.

He looks up. The officer lowers her hand, revealing the GLASS PORCUPINE shimmering in the light. Ralphie slowly grabs hold of it.

RALPHIE
(confused)
This was left behind?

OFFICER MATTHEWS *(O.S.)*
Along with this.

She hands Ralphie a note. It reads: **'Keep this in a box in an attic, someone might try to steal it. - Love, V.M.'** A cartoonish whale is drawn on the side.

Ralphie smiles as he stares at it. A long beat.

RALPHIE
(sotto)
Yeah she would've given me a second.

QUICK FLASHBACK: of the margarita filled glasses colliding together.

CLINK!

CUT TO BLACK

ROLL CREDITS

THE END

THE LEVER DU CINÉ COLLECTION : RENAISSANCE

Fort George Island (1880) by Thomas Moran (1837-1926)

The Bunker
(or, *You Wouldn't Understand*)

Written by

Lever du Ciné

THE BUNKER

The faint sound of rolling thunder.

CUT IN ON

INT. COMMERCIAL AIRLINER – DAY

Turbulence shakes the dimly lit plane. A scruffy looking man (mid30s, ungroomed hair) rests under a tiny spotlight. This is CAL.

The SEATBELT SIGN turns on.

> FLIGHT ATTENDANT MICHELLE *(V.O.)*
> *(over intercomm)*
> Good morning passengers of AirAtlantic flight 216 to Atlanta, Georgia – or rather an almost 'good noon' - we are currently passing through a patch of stormy weather and are expecting to experience a bit of heavy turbulence. The fasten seatbelt sign has been turned on so we ask that you please remain seated until you are once again given the okay to roam around the cabin. We appreciate your co-operation, and thank you as always for choosing to flying with AirAtlantic.

The plane shakes a little bit more. A flight attendant approaches Cal, tapping him on the shoulder.

> F.A. SUSAN *(O.S.)*
> Excuse me sir.
> *(beat)*
> Sir?

A hand from the seat beside shakes Cal.

> EMILY *(O.S.)*
> Baby wake up.

Cal opens his eyes. He turns towards the stewardess.

> F.A. SUSAN *(O.S.)*
> So sorry to wake you, but the fasten seatbelt sign has turned on and I need you to please stow away your seat tray for me.

                    CAL
            Yeah of course.

She points towards his trash.

                F.A. SUSAN
            May I take that from you?

                    CAL
                  Please.

She takes it and moves on as he clicks in his seatbelt and shuts the tray.

Cal turns to his girlfriend, EMILY (early 30s, a kind looking soul).

                    CAL
               How's she been?

                   EMILY
                    Out.

                    CAL
                   Really?

Emily nods. He reaches past her and brushes the face of his baby daughter, ERIN, asleep in a car seat by the window. As he does so, he gets a slight glimpse of the dark stormy skies that surrounds the plane. **THUNDER**.

Cal leans back in his seat and taps on the TV monitor ahead. He opens the live flight tracker – they are about 2 hours of flight time from Atlanta, crossing over the Atlantic Ocean.

The screen glitches. He taps at it in frustration before turning it off.

                   EMILY
              You seem antsy.

                    CAL
                   Do I?

She gives him a slight smile.

THE BUNKER

> CAL
> Yeah I guess being up here makes
> me feel like I should be working.

> EMILY
> I warned you not to pick up that flight
> tomorrow, didn't I? I did say that, no?

> CAL
> You did.

> EMILY
> So?

He exhaustedly looks her in the eyes and mouths, "You were right". She mouths back, "I know".

They share a smile.

> EMILY
> Get to it then.

Cal leans back into his chair, relaxed, ready to fall asleep. A long beat.

BOOM. Lightning flashes close outside the window. The entire plane groans as it shakes forcibly. Passengers are jolted in their seats. They look around as a slight unease arises in the atmosphere. Baby Erin begins to cry.

> EMILY
> *(worrisome)*
> Cal.

She grips his arm.

Cal looks around with the corners of his eyes… feeling the rhythm of the plane. Flight attendants quickly move past him towards the cockpit.

> F.A. MICHELLE *(V.O.)*
> Hello passengers, as you can probably tell we are
> now experiencing severe levels of turbulence, so a reminder
> to please remain in your seats as we continue to pass through
> this patch of weather. The pilots have assured us that all
> is well, and we are expected to be clear in just a few minutes.

Cal looks outside the window. A bizarre red light briefly flashes amidst the stormy clouds.

F.A. SUSAN (V.O.)
If you have any questions please get the
attention of your nearest stewardess and we can –

BOOM! Lightning strikes the right wing, tearing it in half. The engine immediately blows.

Oxygen Masks dropped down as the plane is sent into a vicious downward spin. The passengers scream and panic. Erin bursts into further hysteria.

F.A. MICHELLE (V.O.)
Emergency procedures! Masks on, heads down,
bend forward! Masks on, heads down, bend forward!

After a while the plane joltingly stabilizes but still shakily, and rapidly descends.

CAPTAIN RODGERS (V.O.)
Passengers, this is your Captain speaking,
we are going down! I repeat, *we are going down!* Remain
strapped into your seats and assume emergency positions!

Emily tightly grips Cal's arm, looking to him in fear as she tries to cover their baby.

EMILY	CAL
Cal… Cal… Cal… Cal…!	It's okay, it's okay,
	it's gonna be okay Em –

EMILY
(fearfully)
Cal, *do something!* Cal…!

Cal studies the genuine terror in her eyes, zoning as he stares at her.

CAL
I'll be right back okay? I'm gonna go see what I can do!
You stay in position, you keep your masks on and
you hold her tight, you hear me?! You hold her tight!

THE BUNKER

The ghost-like Emily shakingly nods. Cal unclips his seatbelt and cautiously moves down through the isle towards the front of the descending plane.

The flight attendants are strapped in outside of the cockpit. One frantically speaks into a wall phone. He turns to the approaching Cal.

                  F.A. JOSE
      Sir, sir, sir you need to get back in
        your seat, and into Emergency –

                    CAL
     I'm a pilot with crash landing experience,
      I can help! Tell the captain to let me in!

Jose stares at him in a moment of hesitation amidst the terror. He presses a button and quickly says some words into the phone before again locking eyes with Cal.

                  F.A. JOSE
                    Go.

CLICK. Cal busts through.

INT. COCKPIT – CONTINUOUS

CAPTAIN RODGERS sweats at the controls while CO-PILOT GODDARD speaks vigorously with Atlanta tower control. Cal approaches Rodgers.

              CAPTAIN RODGERS
                 Who are you!

                      CAL
          (rapidly but professionally)
    Cal Weaver, private pilot, former US Air Force
    Sergeant, three successful emergency landings.

              CAPTAIN RODGERS
       The entire right wing is gone –

                    CAL
     I know. Have you done this before?

> CAPTAIN RODGERS
> No I...

Cal notices that the pilot is somewhat unnerved.

> CAL
> You're doing good, okay? That is a graveyard spiral you just recovered us from Captain. You've done incredible work to counteract the spin, now you just need to slowly increase the thrusters and...
> *(beat)*
> Captain?!

Captain Rodgers sits paralyzed behind the controls.

> CAL
> *Captain.*

> CAPTAIN RODGERS
> *(softly)*
> The wing can never go, it's... that's not something that happens... right it's not...? it's...

Cal stares at the petrified man. He turns to look at Co-Pilot Goddard.

> CO-PILOT GODDARD
> *(into headset)*
> ... yes Tower we have no current coordinates... are you hearing me?! No current location, the RADAR is just spinning, we are eastward from our last reported...

Cal turns back to the captain.

> CAL
> Captain, now is not the time to worry about what happened, *this* is what is happening. You've completed the first half of keeping us alive yeah, you're doing just fine, but now you need to quickly lower us below the clouds and then increase the –

> CAPTAIN RODGERS
> There'll be too much turbulence below the storm it's better if we try to maintain our level up –

> CAL
> No Captain. Listen to me: mandates are useless in this now. While we still have some bit of control and momentum, this is our best chance to see if we can spot any sort of land. We need to look for a safe place to attempt to put this down by.

Sweat pours from Captain Rodgers' face as he weighs this up.

Then nervously, he begins lowering the wheel causing further descent. Shouts are heard from the cabin. The altimeter reads **22,000 feet** and dropping.

The stormy clouds and rain blind vision as they breeze past the window…

And then – out of the clouds. The wild ocean below approaches quicker and quicker.

> CAL
> Okay now Captain.

> CAPTAIN RODGERS
> Increasing thrust.

Captain Rodgers slowly pushes forward the thrusters and pulls back hard on the controls. The plane tilts harder, nearly spinning out again.

> CAL
> Aye aye, easy now… easy.

Captain Rodgers stabilizes it. The plummeting altimeter slows a bit.

> CAPTAIN RODGERS
> I got it… I got it. Tell me what you see!

Cal looks out the window to the left, Co-Pilot Goddard to his right. They scan and scan… the altimeter still dropping. Captain Rodgers' eyes frantically dance between it and the still approaching ocean.

> CAPTAIN RODGERS
> I'm gonna need something quick here –

> CO-PILOT GODDARD
> I can't see anything out here Ethan,
> it's just rain and ocean and –

> CAL
> There!

They quickly turn. Cal points – off in the distance, through the rain, the faint outline of an island is visible.

> CAL
> 10 o'clock. I see a small island.

> CAPTAIN RODGERS
> Mike call it in!

> CO-PILOT GODDARD
> *(quickly)*
> Tower, we are preparing for an emergency water landing, we are an estimate of six or seven miles east of wing loss, there is a small island…

> CAPTAIN RODGERS *(O.S.)*
> Cal.

Cal turns to him.

> CAPTAIN RODGERS
> How would you approach this?

Cal eyes dance between the increasingly nearing ocean, and different instruments on the panel. He slips into his head as he thinks. **15,000 feet** and dropping.

> CAL
> We crab it.

> CAPTAIN RODGERS
> Sideways…? Maybe you should take the controls –

> CAL
> No, no. You can do this Captain. You've got this.

Captain Rodgers takes a deep breath as he nods. He slightly lowers the plane, it methodically gains in speed once again.

> CAPTAIN RODGERS
> Goddard, I'ma need you here. Let's dump the gear.

> CO-PILOT GODDARD
> Dumping the gear!

Goddard does accordingly, some added resistance follows.

> CAPTAIN RODGERS
> Okay give me flaps – drop the... drop the flap.

> CO-PILOT GODDARD   CAPTAIN RODGERS
> Full flap.   ... and give me some engine.

> CO-PILOT GODDARD
> Pushing engine!

Goddard does both as Rodgers ever so gently turns the wheel. The planes shakes viciously as the nose begins to turn diagonally, but still remaining on course. **9,000 feet** and dropping.

> CO-PILOT GODDARD *(cont'd)*
> We should be lined up now.

Then Rodgers freezes his hands.

They anxiously sit in silence, transfixed on the swiftly approaching ocean. **5,000 feet** and dropping, the system repeatedly notifying them, *"Too low terrain, too low terrain"*...

> CAPTAIN RODGERS
> Kick the rudder.

> CO-PILOT GODDARD
> Adjusting rudder.

The ship slowly starts to straighten out. The altimeter reads under **1,000 feet**. The plane shakes viciously as it zooms almost inches above the waves, still lowering.

> CAPTAIN RODGERS
> Okay...
> *(into comm)*
> Brace for impact.

They sweat anxiously as they grip tight of whatever they can, waiting in the silence. Cal closes his eyes.

INTERCUT FLASHBACK MEMORY OF EMILY SMILING NEXT TO HIM ON THE PLANE

The system counts down the final few feet... **50... 40... 30...** A large imminent wave emerges directly ahead.

> CAPTAIN RODGERS
> *(into comm)*
> Brace, brace, brace!

IMPACT –

EXT. ATLANTIC OCEAN – CONTINUOUS

The plane violently smashes through the wave and across the ocean's surface before finally coming to a groaning halt.

INT. COCKPIT – CONTINUOUS

The pilots breathe heavily in shock – adrenaline still pumping. <u>Everyone is okay</u>.

A long beat.

> CAL
> You did that Captain.

He rests his hand on Rodgers' shoulder.

> CAL
> Captain you did that.

INT. COMMERCIAL AIRLINER – MOMENTS LATER

The disarrayed passengers moves through the isles towards the emergency exits, ushered by the flight crew. Cal frantically scans all the passengers as they pass him. Finally, Emily rushes towards Cal with Erin in her arms. She bursts into tears as Cal embraces them both.

EMILY
Don't leave me again Cal.

CAL
It's okay sweetie, it's gonna be okay. We're gonna be okay…

Captain Rodgers spots the couple as he continues to direct passengers out.

EMILY
Cal, I'm so scared, I'm so…

CAL
I know baby, I know. It's gonna be okay though.
I'm gonna be right behind you, you hear me? I'll be
in that raft with you. But you've gotta take Erin and
go now so we can get everyone else out, okay?

He kisses her.

EMILY
Okay… Okay…

CAL
I'm gonna be right behind you Em. Go!

She continues moving with the passengers.

Emily holds Erin tight as she looks out over the plane into the endless ocean where the deployed rafts await. She takes a deep breath, covers Erin, and slides down.

SPLASH.

EXT. ATLANTIC OCEAN – MOMENTS LATER

Cal holds Emily close as the convoy of rafts are paddled away from the groaning, submerging plane, and towards the cay-like island.

EXT. THE CAY – DAY

The last of the passengers are escorted off the rafts and onto the shore. They join the rest who huddle in front of the pilots and flight attendants. Murmurs and cries of children fill the group.

CAPTAIN RODGERS
(to F.A. Jose)
Are we sure this is everyone? Are you sure?

F.A. JOSE
Ethan, yes, we've counted several times now, it's exactly –

CAPTAIN RODGERS
And you've matched that to the manifest? Every single person's been checked off and verified on the –

F.A. JOSE
Yes, yes we've accounted for all 67. Everyone is here. Everyone is alive. The worst just being shock and minor injuries but, everyone made it.

CAPTAIN RODGERS
Good… okay, good. Thank God… That's good.

MOTHER PASSENGER	RICH FEMALE PASSENGER
Are you going to tell us what happened!	And is anyone coming for us?

CO-PILOT GODDARD
(lost in thought)
Lightning… struck the right engine causing an explosion. The sheer force of the blast must have ripped the wing clean off… because…

THE BUNKER

    FRUSTRATED MALE   FEMALE COLLEGE
       PASSENGER   STUDENT
       Because what?   Is that something that
                                    can even happen…?

    MIDDLE AGED INDIAN AMERICAN PASSENGER
           What are you guys not telling us!

              CAPTAIN RODGERS
             (trying to speak over)
     The important thing now, okay, is that
   Atlanta Flight Control knows that we have
   gone down and will be sending patrols in the –

   SPANISH PASSENGER   CONCERNED FEMALE
  But do they know exactly   PASSENGER
   where we are though?   Do we know where we
                               are for that matter…

The two pilots exchange a hesitant look between one other as the survivors grow restless. Cal quietly awaits how they will choose to handle this.

             CO-PILOT GODDARD
   They have an approximate idea of the distance between
   the moment we lost the wing and the moment of impact.

Groans and murmurs of concern and unease flood the passengers before he can even finish.

              CAPTAIN RODGERS
   But they also are aware that we will be on an island!
  There is nothing for us to be concerned about, people. We
  have an ample amount of flares and with help most certainly
  already on it's way, we can assure you there's a high likelihood
    of us being rescued in well under 24 hours, God willing.

The passengers all nervously stare at them.

           TEENAGE GIRL PASSENGER
              We're gonna die.

> F.A. MICHELLE
> Hey! Cut that talk.

> FRUSTRATED MALE PASSENGER
> What are we supposed to do then! Just wait out
> in this heat with no food, for God knows how long?

> CAPTAIN RODGERS
> We are not going to die, okay! The hardest part is
> behind us. I mean the fact that we are even here…

He hesitates. As he looks up he spots Cal amidst the crowd.

> CAPTAIN RODGERS
> A huge part of us surviving that is because of the
> knowledge and experience of this young man over here.

He points to him – everyone turns.

> CAPTAIN RODGERS
> He assisted with the emergency landing and
> he is the best equipped to guide us through
> this next portion of getting back home. Cal?

Everyone stares, waiting. Emily rubs his arm.

> CAL
> Hi… yeah, my name is Cal Weaver, I'm a private
> pilot and former Staff Sergeant of the US Air Force,
> with three successful emergency landings. Call it bad
> luck but I guess this makes that three and a half.

An awkward chuckle come from within the crowd.

> CAL *(cont'd)*
> I'm uh… I'm here with my girlfriend Emily and my baby
> girl Erin. And I want to get them home, just as badly as
> you do with yours. I feel your frustrations, I do… but this is
> the situation we are in; this is the reality. Now A.T.L. and the
> national guard know what has happened. They are professionals
> trained for these situations – *they will find us*. But our survival
> takes two; now's the time to put all our concerns to the
> side and do our part. Everyone needs to chip in.

                    CAL *(cont'd)*
It would be wise to split into groups and sort out the basics:
food, drinkable water, rations, shelter, signal fire. As the Captain
has already stated we can expect to be found in under 24 hours,
but in our heads we have to be prepared for the possibility that we
could be here longer. Regardless, everything is going to be okay
as long as we work together, remain calm, and stay optimistic.

He stands in thought for a moment.

                    CAL *(cont'd)*
We shouldn't be alive. I know that's not something that should
be said, but it's true. Us being here now... *this* is a miracle.
Let's do what we have to do so the world knows that.

The group of survivors seem a little more at ease. Captain Rodgers nods to Cal.

                    CAPTAIN RODGERS
Thank you for that Cal. Let's get to it then people. Our flight
crew will organize splitting you up into groups to scour the
land and gather any resources that might assist our
survival and eventual rescue. Michelle if you would –

                    RICH FEMALE PASSENGER
What about those of us with injuries?
I'm bleeding down my leg.

                    TEENAGE GIRL PASSENGER
Yeah I think I have a concussion too.

                    CAPTAIN RODGERS
Right, do we have a doctor by any chance?

A woman raises her hand.

                    NURSE PASSENGER
I'm a nurse.

                    CAPTAIN RODGERS
That's perfect. If you are injured or feel unable,
come to the rafts and we'll treat you as best as
we can there. Alright, let's get moving.

A portion of passengers break off from the group towards the rafts while Cal and the majority stick with the flight attendants who begin shouting instructions.

> CAPTAIN RODGERS (O.S.)
> Cal.

Cal turns to the captain now beside him.

> CAPTAIN RODGERS
> Do you mind helping with injuries?
> We could use your service experience there too.

Cal looks to Emily. She hesitantly nods for him to go.

> CAL
> Yeah.

> CAPTAIN RODGERS
> Thank you Cal.

Cal breaks off with him and follows the group towards the rafts. Flight Attendant Susan joins up with the two.

> F.A. SUSAN
> You know something, I can't seem to tell if the
> storm is coming or going... or if it's just sitting there.

Cal looks towards the storm, still raging in the distance.

EXT. THE CAY – DAY

SERIES OF DISSOLVING SHOTS: Cal helps with patching up the injured survivors. Emily and others scour the island in their groups, collecting branches, and eventually starting a fire.

EXT. SHORE, THE CAY – DAY

Cal finishes helping his last passenger. He walks over to the sea and bends down, washing the blood off of his hands and splashing water onto his face. He sits there for a moment, deep in thought.

THE BUNKER

> CAPTAIN RODGERS *(O.S.)*
> Hey.

Cal looks up to see the Captain. He tosses him a miniature bottle of water. Cal opens it and takes some sips.

> CAL
> Thanks.

They stay there silent for moment, watching the storm.

> CAPTAIN RODGERS
> Hey about what went on up there in the flight deck –

> CAL
> Don't. I've come to learn that in the end of it those things don't matter. Only to ego but… you did the job, Captain.

Cal looks to him, they share a soft smile. Rodgers' smile emptily fades.

> CAPTAIN RODGERS
> That's just not something that…
> *(beat)*
> The wing. That's just not something that happens.

The two men sit in silence.

> CAL
> I know.

Intense rustling comes from the brush behind them. They turn to the noise, alerted.

Flight Attendant Jose and two other passengers push out through the brush toward them.

> F.A. JOSE
> *(catching his breath)*
> Rodgers… you need to…

> CAPTAIN RODGERS
> What's going on Jose.

> F.A. JOSE
> We found something.

> CAPTAIN RODGERS
> Okay, what. What?

> F.A. JOSE
> Ethan, you should come see this.

Cal and Rodgers stare at him, curiously.

INT. INLAND, THE CAY - DAY

WORM'S EYE VIEW: Jose, Cal and Rodgers slowly emerge, looking down towards the "something" in question.

> CAPTAIN RODGERS
> It's a storm shelter?

> CAL
> It's a bunker.

An OLD STEEL DOOR is built in amidst the sand and brush. Looks of pure perplexity fill their faces.

> CAPTAIN RODGERS
> Have you tried opening it?

> F.A. JOSE
> You must be joking.

Rustling grows around them. Rodgers looks up.

> CAPTAIN RODGERS
> How many people have seen this?

> F.A. JOSE
> Just a few from our group...

> CAPTAIN RODGERS
> Because I'm thinking it might be better if we keep this hush hush until we know for sure what we're…

THE BUNKER

A mass of passengers flood in through the brush to see the bizarre spectacle. Emily is with them.

> CAPTAIN RODGERS
> *(sotto)*
> Well.

Murmurs of questions and concerns flood the passengers.

> CAPTAIN RODGERS
> Alright let's not get worked up over —

> BLACK MALE PASSENGER
> What the hell is an underground bunker doing on a remote island in the middle of the Atlantic?

> CONCERNED FEMALE PASSENGER
> Did anyone see any people around the island not with us?

> F.A. JOSE
> Sir we do not know we are just as confused as —

> SPANISH PASSENGER
> Maybe it's been abandoned.

> INDIAN AMERICAN PASSENGER
> Why would anyone build a bunker on an island just to abandon it though?

> CAPTAIN RODGERS
> Everyone please can we just —

> CAL
> *(loudly)*
> It's most likely just old military.

A beat. Everyone quiets as they consider this.

> EMILY
> Yeah but who's?

More unspoken unease.

> MALE COLLEGE STUDENT
> Has anyone tried going in?

> FRUSTRATED MALE PASSENGER
> Are you mental?

> **MALE COLLEGE STUDENT**
> It's just a bunker.

> **FRUSTRATED MALE PASSENGER**
> Yeah and we have no clue who or what could be in there!

> **NURSE PASSENGER**
> Exactly, we have no clue what is in there, and it could be food, water, medical supplies, more resources –

> **MOTHER PASSENGER**
> Why should we be worried about those things, we won't be stuck here long anyway –

> **CONCERNED FEMALE PASSENGER**
> Or maybe there could be a reason they've closed in whatever's in there!

> **RICH FEMALE PASSENGER**
> I agree!

> **MALE PROFESSOR**
> It can't hurt to look.

> **NURSE PASSENGER**
> And if anything it could offer some shade for the children and the elderly.

> **BLACK MALE PASSENGER**
> What we need to do is go to the shore and wait by the signal fire with the rest of us.

> **CAPTAIN RODGERS**
> Everyone, please! We all need to slow down for a moment and just pick ourselves up, okay? We need some order here.

A faint muffled sound grows from the bunker...

> **CAPTAIN RODGERS**
> *(getting distracted)*
> Now we all can certainly agree that our priority remains with getting rescued and off this island, so there is no need for us to make any rash decisions on this here, and we needn't – we need... we needn't worry our... ourselves...

The group silence as they stare towards the door. From far inside, *"Pick Yourself Up"* by Frank Sinatra echoes faintly. Looks of discomfort are shared.

> **F.A. SUSAN**
> Was that music always playing?

They all stare at the door. A beat.

EXT. INLAND, THE CAY – MOMENTS LATER

Cal, the pilots, and a few passengers work together to spin the rusty lock and pull open the heavy door.

The echoing music bounces up through the long, pitch black staircase. They stare down into it. A beat.

> AUTISTIC TEENAGE PASSENGER
> I saw this old show once and there was a bunker on the island and it had this doomsday button that turned out to be the reason the people crashed on the island in the first place.
> *(beat)*
> I guess I should mentioned that the show was about people who survived a plane crash just like –

> F.A. MICHELLE
> Okay that's enough of that talk thank you...

They all still stare, nervously paralyzed. Another beat of silence.

> RICH FEMALE PASSENGER
> Hello!

Her shout of "Hello" echoes down in.

> F.A. JOSE
> Shh!

> FRUSTRATED MALE PASSENGER
> Are you stupid?!

> RICH FEMALE PASSENGER
> What?

> F.A. SUSAN
> We don't know who's down there.

> RICH FEMALE PASSENGER
> How bad can they be, they like Sinatra.

> **FRUSTRATED MALE PASSENGER**
> Yeah and when whoever's down their comes up and
> shoots and cooks us all and uses our bones as —

> **F.A. MICHELLE**
> Hey, hey!

> **MOTHER PASSENGER**
> Jesus...

> **CO-PILOT GODDARD**
> Aye, watch it!

> **FRUSTRATED MALE PASSENGER**
> Then you'll see, then we'll see!

> **BLACK MALE PASSENGER**
> We told your ass to quit that talk man there are children!

The echo of the Rich Female Passenger's *"Hi"* travels back up.

> **FRUSTRATED MALE PASSENGER**
> What? I'm only trying to be realistic here.

> **F.A. MICHELLE**
> You're not helping anything sir so if you can't watch
> your mouth you should to go on back to the beach.

> **FRUSTRATED MALE PASSENGER**
> This is free land I can do whatever I please...

> **RICH FEMALE PASSENGER**
> Hey shut it! Shut up!

They quiet. She points towards the bunker.

> **RICH FEMALE PASSENGER**
> I did not say that.

> **FRUSTRATED MALE PASSENGER**
> What do you mean you didn't say that, that sounds
> like your annoying ass voice over and over again to me!

> **RICH FEMALE PASSENGER**
> I said "Hello" you nit, that echo coming back is saying
> 'Hi'... but it sounds exactly like me and I didn't say that...

Everyone stares in.

CAPTAIN RODGERS
Hello is anyone in there?

His echo bounces as it disappears down the stairs. They wait. Then, the echoes slowly travel back towards them.

ECHOING VOICE
(sounding exactly alike)
Hi I'm in here... Hi I'm in here... Hi I'm in here...!
Hi I'm in here...! Hi I'm in here! Hi I'm in here!

They stare, confused and uneased.

CAPTAIN RODGERS
(nervously)
Are you okay down there?

His voice travels down. Then it returns.

ECHOING VOICE
(distorted)
Help... Help... Help...! Help...! Help...!
Help...! Me! Help! Me! Help! Me! Help me!

EXT. INLAND, THE CAY – MOMENTS LATER

Cal quickly grabs a branch and rips off a piece of his shirt, tying it around it.

FRUSTRATED MALE PASSENGER
We can still close the door man and wait to
be rescued, we don't have to go in there...

Co-Pilot Goddard grabs a few flares, handing them out.

RICH FEMALE PASSENGER
Yeah for once I agree with the little angry guy.

F.A. SUSAN
Captain, I'm not sure a lot of us are comfortable
going down in there with the concerns of –

CAPTAIN RODGERS
That's fine Susan, only the people who want to be of service need to come, the rest of you can stay outside or go back to the beach and wait for us to return.

F.A. SUSAN
Yes but, Ethan... something doesn't feel right here...

They continue to go back and forth. Cal stands at the mouth of the bunker. He pours a travel size bottle of alcohol on his makeshift torch. Emily approaches him, rocking Erin.

EMILY
I'm coming with you.

CAL
No Em, no you are not.

EMILY
Yes, I am Cal, you don't get to –

CAL
Em, don't do this now, please just –

EMILY
(sharp whisper)
Cal, there may be trouble ahead in there and you promised me, *you promised me* that we were sticking together until we –

CAL
Baby, it's just an old bunker! It's just a normal god damn bunker. We are going to check to see if someone's hurt down there and then I'll be –

EMILY
Listen Calvin!

She points towards the bunker. Cal notices that the song coming from deep inside has changed, now playing *"Let's Face the Music and Dance"* by *Frank Sinatra*.

THE BUNKER

> EMILY
> That's not normal Cal, someone is playing music
> from the words that I am speaking to you!

Cal stares down as he contemplates.

> CAL
> Em, it's gonna be okay, just –

> EMILY
> Why can't you just tell me what's really going
> on in your head? Why can't you just say things? Huh?

Cal continues to stare inside, lost in a permeating thought.

> CAL
> You wouldn't understand.

A beat.

> EMILY
> Calvin...

> CAL
> Please baby, I need you to wait here. These people are trusting
> me to keep them safe down there if anything happens –
> *which it won't*, and one of us needs to be here for her!

Emily goes to speak but catches herself. She looks back with the corner of her eye – some close by have overheard the argument.

> CAL
> All three of us survived the impossible together Em.
> And I'm not prepared for the possibility of failing
> with both your lives in my hands. You hear me?

She reluctantly nods.

> CAL
> Yeah?
> *(to F.A. Jose)*
> Jose, you keep an eye on them
> for me until we get back, okay?

                    F.A. JOSE
                  Yes, of course.

Captain Rodgers approaches him, looking down the stairway.

                  CAPTAIN RODGERS
                      Here.

He hands him a PISTOL. Emily watches the transaction as she reluctantly steps away.

                       CAL
                     Cockpit?

Rodgers nods.

                  CAPTAIN RODGERS
              You're probably the most qualified
                to use it... should we need it.

Cal looks at the gun and nods before tucking it into his pants.

The rest of the entering party – Co-Pilot Goddard, the Nurse, the Male Professor, and the Frustrated Male Passenger – join the two at the mouth of the bunker. They stare down within.

              FRUSTRATED MALE PASSENGER
                   Well... After y'all.

Cal lights the torch.

                       CAL
                   Stay close now.

INT. THE BUNKER – MOMENTS LATER

The group tail close behind Cal and his sole source of light as they move through a pitch black tunnel. No visible light ahead, the faint daylight cast down the stairs behind them slowly shrinking. *"Santa Clause is Coming to Town" by Frank Sinatra* plays far in the distance, chopping sporadically.

THE BUNKER

>   NURSE PASSENGER
>   I don't know how anyone could stand
>   living in this for Lord knows how long.
>
>   MALE PROFESSOR
>   If anyone is exposed to this length of darkness,
>   there's an increased likelihood of psychological distress...
>
>   FRUSTRATED MALE PASSENGER
>   Right because who listens to
>   Christmas music in the middle of May.
>
>   CO-PILOT GODDARD
>   Maybe they don't know what month it is.

They travel further in, the music never seeming to draw nearer.

>   CAPTAIN RODGERS
>   *(calling out)*
>   Hello? Can you still hear me?

His voice travels down the hallway. They continue walking.

The echo returns.

>   ECHOING VOICE (V.O.)
>   Hi, I can hear you... Hi, I can hear you... Hi I can
>   hear you...! Hi I can hear you! Hi I can hear you!
>
>   FRUSTRATED MALE PASSENGER
>   Well where are you, dammit?! Show yourself!

The voice travels down. Then, it travels back. But this time, the voice quickly comes from all around them.

>   ECHOING VOICE (V.O.)
>   I'mLeftI'mRightI'mForwardI'mDiagonalI'mRight
>   I'mToTheNorth InTheEastCorridorI'mInTheSmallPassageToTheSide...!
>   I'mLeftI'mRightI'mForwardI'mDiagonalI'mRight
>   I'mToTheNorthInTheEastCorridorI'mInTheSmallPassageToTheSide!
>   *(beat)*
>   Dammit!

They all freeze. Cal spins the flame around revealing multiple hallways splitting up from where they now stand. The group stares down the dark tunnels – <u>there is one for each of them.</u>

Cal looks back. The daylight is all but a speck.

>CAPTAIN RODGERS
>Okay… Okay so we each take our flares and pick a path, and –

>FRUSTRATED MALE PASSENGER
>Hell no, *hell no* I'm not splitting off
>from no one in this hell scape of a –

>CAPTAIN RODGERS
>Hey! In case you haven't noticed: noise travels!
>You see something, you call out, we come to you.

The Frustrated Male Passenger restlessly weighs this up.

>FRUSTRATED MALE PASSENGER
>Alright but I'm looking down and then
>I'm out of here you hear me? Huh?

>NURSE PASSENGER
>Why would you offer to come if
>you were just going to complain –

>FRUSTRATED MALE PASSENGER
>Oh you think that I'm an asshole huh just because
>I seem to be the only one willing to admit that –

>CO-PILOT GODDARD
>*Alright already.*

Captain Rodgers lights his flare and looks at all the tunnels, before landing on one.

>CAPTAIN RODGERS
>Call if you see anything.

He proceeds into it.

THE BUNKER

>   CAL
>   I'll leave the torch here should you need
>   to find your way back to this spot.

>   MALE PROFESSOR
>   Okay, so... Who takes what?

The Frustrated Male Passenger lights his flare and looks down a hall.

>   FRUSTRATED MALE PASSENGER
>   If I find treasure, it's mine...

He disappears down. The rest light their flares, pick a path, and one by one disappear in, leaving Cal and the flame behind.

He looks back one last time –

EXT. INLAND, THE CAY – SIMULTANEOUSLY

Emily anxiously stares down into the bunker.

INT. THE BUNKER – SIMULTANEOUSLY

Cal turns to his path. He enters, disappearing within.

Now, just the burning flame.

INT. CAL'S TUNNEL, THE BUNKER – MOMENTS LATER

Cal walks through the pitch black tunnel. *"Strangers in the Night" by Frank Sinatra* now plays close ahead.

As he nears the sound of the music, a GRAMOPHONE appears at the edge of his light in the middle of the hallway. Cal approaches it.

He looks ahead – nothing but darkness. As he reaches down for the needle the music suddenly begins to chop in place.

>   FRANK SINATRA *(V.O.)*
>   Up... Up... Up Up Up Up!

Cal listens for a moment... thinking. Then rapidly he shines his light to the ceiling.

Directly above him is an elaborately detailed CAVE-LIKE PAINTING – of two cavemen hunting by a river (sketched as if they are being observed). One is hairier, the other darker skinned.

The music spins out.

Cal proceeds forward – there is another etched painting on the ceiling. The darker skinned caveman is enthusiastic from having caught a fish.

Cal moves forward to see another – the same image is enhanced on the face of the hairier caveman. He stares at the fish, covetously.

Cal proceeds quicker now. In the next image above – the darker skinned caveman cooks his fish on a fire.

In the next – the hairier caveman stands over the other, with a large rock held over his head.

In the next – the hairier caveman smashes it into the darker skinned caveman's head. Blood flies up.

In the next image – he raises his hands.

In the next – he smashes it in again. More blood.

In the next image – he raises his hands.

And in then the next – he smashes it in again.

In the following painting – the hairier caveman, covered in blood, sits by the fire eating the fish, next to the corpse of the darker skinned caveman.

And in the one after that – he has finished the fish. He sits staring at the dead caveman, his face is heavy with confliction. Cal stops and stares at this image.

Then on to the next one – the hairier caveman wanders along the river.

Then the next one – the hairier caveman wanders along the river.

Then the next one – the hairier caveman wanders along the river.

Finally – the man comes across another caveman, hunting by the river. He too is covered in blood. They stare at each other, cautiously.

Cal lingers on this.

SUDDENLY – loud bare footsteps rapidly approach Cal from ahead. He quickly reaches for the gun. From the darkness ahead, a CAVEMAN (covered in blood, dressed in human bones) rapidly emerges into the flare light sprinting towards him, carrying a LARGE ROCK above his head. As Cal quickly backs up, he slips, falling onto his back. The gun slides across the floor out of reach.

Cal stares petrified as the caveman stops over him, breathing animalistically, with a cold fury in his eyes.

A beat.

The caveman slams the rock down into Cal's skull. Blood splatters upward. He slams it in repeatedly.

EXT. INLAND, THE CAY – SIMULTANEOUSLY

A group of the passengers who stayed behind wait around the bunker entrance.

Rapid rustling comes from the brush around.

> FEMALE COLLEGE STUDENT *(O.S.)*
> Hey!

Those around the bunker turn.

> FEMALE COLLEGE STUDENT *(O.S.)*
> Helicopter...!

She pushes through the brush to them.

> FEMALE COLLEGE STUDENT
> *(catching her breath)*
> They've found us... there's a helicopter coming right for... us, coming from the –

Life fills the passengers faces.

> F.A. JOSE
> Alright, everyone get to the beach, now!

> RICH FEMALE PASSENGER
> Oh my god, finally...

> EMPATHETIC PASSENGER
> What about the people still in there?

> F.A. JOSE
> *(fading)*
> I will stay and wait for them. You all just get back to
> the shore and let them know that we still have...

Emily zones out the chatter as she nervously stares deep into the bunker, rocking her baby girl.

INT. THE BUNKER – DAY

Cal (unscaved) walks through the dark hallway. *"Strangers in the Night" by Frank Sinatra* plays far ahead.

He holds his flare to the walls – there are tally marks painted in dry blood, getting less and less frantic the further he travels in.

A sudden scream echoes from far behind him. Cal quickly looks back. He grips the gun as he turns and listens.

> ECHOING VOICE *(V.O.)*
> Cal, Cal, bring the gun! Come
> here now Cal! Bring the –

More screams of panic.

> CAL
> I'm coming, where are you!

No reply. Just screams.

THE BUNKER

> CAL
> I'm coming right now just keep talking so I can —

A loud noise of rustling chains comes from nearby ahead. Cal rapidly draws the pistol forward as he shines the light.

At the edge of the reach of his flare sits a SMALL FIGURE huddled in the shadows.

Cal slowly approaches it. As he draws nearer, he hears the faint sound of weeping. Cal cocks the pistol.

The figure's head immediately looks up. Then, it stands and approaches him, chain dragging behind. As the being draws nearer to Cal, his face is filled with discomfort.

The figure is a SMALL DECREPIT MAN — his eyes abnormally placed, his body obtuse and swollen.

> DECREPIT MAN
> My inside's hurt...

> CAL
> What are... What are you doing
> down here? Are you okay?

> DECREPIT MAN
> No... I've been chained in here for so long...
> and my insides burn... for so long...

> CAL
> There is a... we came with a
> nurse back there... she may...

The decrepit man grabs hold of him.

> DECREPIT MAN
> *(crying)*
> They've rearranged me so many times...

> CAL
> Who did this to you? What's down here?

> DECREPIT MAN
> You need to get me out of here, I wanna see the –

The sound of a door opening ahead. The music blasts louder. Cal looks down to the decrepit man, who's wonky eyes widen with fear.

> DECREPIT MAN
> *Run.*

THREE LANKY, FACELESS ALIEN CREATURES swiftly emerge from the darkness, grabbing them both, dragging them separately into the darkness.

INT. SURGICAL ROOM, THE BUNKER – CONTINUOUS

Cal kicks and screams as he is dragged through into a dimly lit surgical room and forced onto an advancedly designed table.

The aliens pin down his arm and legs until they lock into the device.

> CAL
> *(frantically)*
> No, no, no... Please...! Please!
> *(calling out)*
> Help! Help me! Stop please –

An alien flips on slicing equipment that loudly masks his screams. Cal's body convulses as the device gets lower and closer...

CONTACT –

INT. CAL'S TUNNEL, THE BUNKER – PRIOR

Cal (a little more weary) walks through the tunnel, with his sole source of light. *"Strangers in the Night" by Frank Sinatra* plays far ahead. Multiple screams come from behind. Cal looks back.

Suddenly – a rat scurries past his feet, startling him. He shines his light ahead again, attentively. Cal grips the gun as he ignores the cries and curiously presses forward.

He walks... the music drawing nearer... and then at the end of the reach of his light – a wall appears directly ahead. <u>The tunnel is a dead end</u>. The music blasts from a speaker hung overhead.

The puzzled Cal approaches the wall. He stares emptily for a moment.

>   CAL
>   No, no, no...

Cal pushes at the wall. He hits it harder and harder as his frustration amounts.

>   CAL
>   *(furiously)*
>   No! This doesn't make sense! It can't be it!
>   This isn't it! What the hell are we here for –

INT. CAL'S TUNNEL, THE BUNKER – PRIOR

Cal's face is much wearier as he anxiously walks down the dark hallway. Multiple screams come from far behind him, yet he remains persistently trained ahead. Strangers in the Night by Frank Sinatra plays, drawing nearer.

>   CAL
>   *(sotto)*
>   Come on... come on...

He walks and walks... until he sees it – at the end of the hall, is a door with light just barely seeping under. Cal approaches it. He clinches the gun as he slowly leans in to listen... nothing on the other side but music.

Cal breathes as he composes himself. He aims the gun and bursts through –

INT. CONTROL ROOM, THE BUNKER – CONTINUOUS

A dimly lit control room with hundreds of blank camera monitors. There is no one in sight.

Cal cautiously approaches the control panel. As he looks over it, a massive red buttons catches his eyes. It is labeled - **You Wouldn't Understand**. The befuddled Cal contemplates for a moment. Then, he pushes it.

The music cuts out, a light flashes red, and one single center monitor lights up. Footage plays on it of an exterior perspective of his entire PLANE CRASH (taken as if being observed). Then, footage of the survivors rafting to the island away from the sinking plane. Then of them scouring the island. Then of them entering into the bunker.

SUDDENLY, all the monitors light up. They all play the same recording – of Cal walking though the dark tunnel. But as they continue, each of them captures a different scenario from then on.

Cal stares, overwhelmed. The cavemen, decrepit man, and dead end scenarios each play on their own screen, surrounded by hundreds of different scenarios (some more fantastical than others), each ending so unsatisfyingly for the Cal they capture. Then, they loop back to him walking.

>   CAL
>   (sotto)
>   What is this…?

As Cal's eyes rapidly dance across the looping monitors, they lock on to one in particular. His face becomes ghost-like.

EMILY (seen on one single monitor) has entered down into the bunker, nervously trekking through the dark. Cal's heart races as he backs up and sprints out of the control room.

A beat. All the monitors fade off, EXCEPT for the one fixed on Emily.

INT. THE BUNKER – MOMENTS LATER

Cal sprints back through the dark tunnel. Deep screams still sound around the bunker. He spots the light of the intersection. A figure stands over the torch, picking it up.

>   CAL
>   Hey!

The body turns – it is Emily. He sprints harder towards her.

>   CAL
>   Em what are you doing down here?!

He grabs hold of her.

> CAL
> Are you okay?

She stares at him blankly, just breathing.

> CAL
> Where's Erin?

She continues to stare at him blankly. He takes the torch and hugs her tightly.

> CAL
> It's alright baby, okay? It's gonna be okay, but I'm gonna need you to tell me right now: where did you leave –

> EMILY *(O.S.)*
> Cal…?

Cal freezes. He looks up – EMILY is standing a few feet away from them to the direction of entrance. She stares, mortified.

Cal is paralyzed in fear. Slowly he pulls the being off of him, until they are face to face. A devilish smile stretches across the mouth of the Emily Look-alike.

> EMILY LOOK-ALIKE
> *(lifelessly)*
> Where's Erin? Where's Erin?

A beat. Quickly Cal draws the gun. **BANG!** Emily screams at the sound of the gunshot.

The Emily Look-alike's face never changes as she slowly slumps into Cal's arms. He stares into her eyes, terrified, yet conflictingly emotional. Slowly, the look-alike breaks into a choked laughter.

> EMILY
> *(lifelessly)*
> You've already believed this… We've already got you…

She continues to laugh emotionlessly, softer and softer until – silence.

Cal looks up to Emily, both breathing heavily.

EXT. INLAND, THE CAY – MOMENTS LATER

Cal pulls Emily quickly through the brush.

>   EMILY
>   Cal…
>
>   CAL
>   Where's Erin, Em?

Her face is ghost-like.

>   CAL
>   Em! Where's Erin?!
>
>   EMILY
>   The beach… she's by the beach…
>
>   CAL
>   Okay… Come on…

EXT. SHORE, THE CAY – MOMENTS LATER

The two burst out of the brush onto the beach where all the survivors crowd around a military helicopter.

F.A. SUSAN	F.A. MICHELLE
Women and children,	Please do not push or fight, there
first please…	will be more helicopters on their
	way, we are all getting rescued.

>   CAL
>   Jose!

Cal pushes through the crowd in search of the flight attendant.

>   CAL *(cont'd)*
>   Jose!

He spots Jose organizing people with baby Erin in one arm. He and Emily rush over to him.

Cal takes her back. He holds her and Emily in a moment of comfort. Emily cries. Relief falls on Cal's face.

> FEMALE COLLEGE STUDENT *(O.S.)*
> There's more! Look there's three
> more over there, on their way!

Cal and Emily look up – from the East, three more choppers fly in the distance, headed right for them.

The passengers celebrate in a moment of glee. Cal smiles.

INTERCUT SHOT OF THE BUNKER DOOR LEFT WIDE OPEN

The smile fades from Cal's face, replaced by terror.

> CAL
> Come on.

He takes Emily by her arm and quickly leads them towards the helicopter.

> EMILY
> Cal...

The Helicopter pilot (wearing a dark helmet over his face) helps Emily climb aboard where other women and children await. Cal hands her Erin.

> CAL
> I'll see you at land sweetie okay? I'll be right –

> EMILY
> Cal, Cal, no Cal, please just leave
> with us, I won't go without –

> CAL
> Em, Em! It's okay now. *We are safe*. I will
> be right behind you. Don't split with Erin, and
> I will find you back home. *I promise you.*

Em stares at him with a sorrowful uncertainty.

                    EMILY
            Cal, what was that down there?

Cal stares back as he breathes and breathes.

                    CAL
                I love you Em.

She likewise stares back.

                    EMILY
              I love you too Cal.

They kiss. Cal backs away and gives the helicopter pilot a thumbs up. The pilot slowly reciprocates. He closes the door.

Cal watches the helicopter rise into the air before turning and running into the brush. The helicopter flies westward towards the storm.

EXT. INLAND, THE CAY – MOMENTS LATER

Cal sprints through the brush towards the bunker.

As he approaches, a hand reaches out. Cal freezes, quickly drawing his gun towards it.

Slowly, Captain Rodgers pulls himself out of the bunker. He is bleeding in his lower half.

              CAPTAIN RODGERS
        Cal, oh thank goodness. I got attacked
             by something in there and I –

                    CAL
                 Don't move!

He keeps the gun trained on him.

              CAPTAIN RODGERS
              Cal it's okay it's me –

                    CAL
            Where is everyone else!

CAPTAIN RODGERS
I don't know... all I heard was screams... and then nothing. I think they're dead Cal, I think they're –

CAL
How do you know?

CAPTAIN RODGERS
Because they weren't calling back to me. Just music, and screams... and... and I got lost and things weren't making sense to me and...

He starts to cry. He reaches out.

CAPTAIN RODGERS
You gotta help me Cal –

CAL
What's your name?

CAPTAIN RODGERS
Cal, what do mean, what are you –

CAL
(yelling)
What's your name, what is your name! You're going to need to convince me that you are –

CAPTAIN RODGERS
Cal, it's me, we both went in there, we both survived the crash –

Cal cocks the pistol.

CAL
(aggressively)
Hey!

CAPTAIN RODGERS
(frantically)
My name is Ethan Rodgers, I live in Syracuse, New York, I have a wife and three beautiful children, I am a pilot I –

BANG! Captain Rodgers drops dead. Cal stands frozen, gun still aimed. A beat.

Cal kicks the lifeless Captain Rodgers down into the bunker before closing the door and spinning in the lock. He hurries off into the brush.

The bunker sits silently. Then, from deep within… the beginning of *"We'll Meet Again" by Frank Sinatra* faintly echoes.

INT. SHORE, THE CAY – MOMENTS LATER

Cal burst towards the shore. The last survivors climb into a helicopter, ushered by flight attendants Jose and Susan. Cal approaches them.

> F.A. JOSE
> Cal! Where are the others, did they…

Cal reservedly shakes his head. Jose stares at him horrified.

> F.A. JOSE
> Oh my god… we need to get out of here now.
> *(to pilot)*
> Pilot! This is everyone!

Cal looks at the cay one last time before shutting the doors to the chopper.

EXT. THE CAY – CONTINUOUS

The helicopters lift off one by one, flying eastward. Cal moves over to the pilots' side.

> CAL
> *(over the flight noise)*
> Hey! Why are we flying a different route!

> HELICOPTER PILOT
> What?

> CAL
> *(louder)*
> Why are we flying a different path than the first one!

THE BUNKER

> HELICOPTER PILOT
> I don't know what you're talking about! We came with these three!

> CAL
> No, you –

A beat. Cal's face slowly sinks. The life in him drains, replaced by sheer terror.

INTERCUT FLASHBACK MEMORY OF THE MASKED HELICOPTER PILOT GIVING HIM A THUMBS UP

Cal breathing increases. His heart races.

> CAL
> No…

He looks back towards the storm.

Tears well in his eyes, Cal goes to scream –

EXT. ATLANTIC OCEAN – CONTINUOUS

Cal's screams are inaudible as the helicopters fly further away from the cay. The storm rages off in the distance.

RED LIGHTNING strikes.

CUT TO BLACK

MUSIC CUE: ['WE'LL MEET AGAIN' BY FRANK SINATRA]

ROLL CREDITS

THE END

À BIENTÔT

Lever du Ciné

Printed in Great Britain
by Amazon

b9c1d1aa-c77b-47c9-afbd-e52e575dd917R02